THE SURVIVALIST 7
THE PROPHET

The infra-red seeker confirme
already detected – crosses wit.
them, at the edge of the valley surrounding the base as
he swept over at mach point five. He rolled the plane
into a steep right bank, pulling up and climbing,
arming his weapons systems – Sidewinder missiles and
the gun. Leveling out, he switched the seeker system
from infra-red to television, setting his weapons-
control panel off computer and to manual – it was
somehow more personal when done by hand.

He kept his speed down, cutting off his climb,
leveling out, then starting to dive, the television
camera below him in the fuselage behind the nose on
maximum resolution, picking up what appeared to be
at least a thousand of the wildmen, perhaps more,
massing.

He released the arming safety switch – ready.

He worked the button.

There was a rush, a roar, a buzzing sound and a
contrail of smoke, the Sidewinder from portside at the
fuselage rear firing, tracking into the crowd of insane
non-humans.

Rourke pulled up the nose, the explosion belching
white smoke beneath him. He started the craft to
climb, leveling off then and banking into a roll,
hearing some of the cargo slightly shift but not move,
leveling out. The next missile armed – he started
down ...

*The Survivalist series by Jerry Ahern published
by New English Library:*

1: TOTAL WAR
2: THE NIGHTMARE BEGINS
3: THE QUEST
4: THE DOOMSAYER
5: THE WEB
6: THE SAVAGE HORDE
7: THE PROPHET

THE SURVIVALIST 7
THE PROPHET

Jerry Ahern

NEW ENGLISH LIBRARY

First published in the USA in 1984 by Kensington Publishing Corporation

Copyright © 1984 by Jerry Ahern

First NEL Paperback Edition April 1985

NEL Books are published by
New English Library,
Mill Road, Dunton Green,
Sevenoaks, Kent.
Editorial office: 47 Bedford Square, London WC1B 3DP

Printed and bound in Great Britain by
Cox & Wyman Ltd, Reading

British Library C.I.P.

Ahern, Jerry
  The prophet.–(The Survivalist; 7)
  I. Title   II. Series
  813′.54 F   PS35S1.H4/

  ISBN 0–450–05811–5

For Jerry Kushnick—a good agent, a good friend . . .

Chapter One

The climb down from the rocks to their base had been hard—hard for Natalia whose skin color was still too pale, arduous for the wounded as well. Rourke again carried Natalia's M-16, Rubenstein her pack. Cole and his two men had hung back, a rear guard against a further attack by the wildmen, but judging from the primitive quality of their actions, Rourke doubted the wildmen would come nearer the valley—at lease not until it was realized that he and the others could travel the valley safely and not die from radiation—Rourke hoped.

Well ahead of them, Paul walked, the wand of the Geiger counter extended ahead of him, his voice occasionally singing back an all clear. The only danger would be a freak combining of isotopes during the small conventional blasts needed to trigger the neutron release—and if Paul Rubenstein did find a hot spot, by the time he had the reading on his Geiger counter it would be too late to save himself, given the lack of availability of any decontamination equipment.

Rourke walked on, Natalia beside him. "Go with Paul," she whispered, interrupting his thoughts.

"You want to be with Paul—in case. I know that. I would, too—go ahead."

He glanced at her, reaching out his right arm, his CAR-15 between their bodies—and he folded his arm about her waist to support her.

"I am all right," she nodded.

"Bullshit," he whispered quietly.

He craned his neck to look over his right shoulder, shouting to Lieutenant O'Neal and the others behind them, "Veer off toward that small canyon over on the left—we can rest there."

"I don't need to rest," she whispered.

"Yes, you do," he told her, then ignored her, calling out to Rubenstein ahead of them, the younger man turning around, "Paul—pull back—head toward that small canyon—get some rest!"

"Gotchya," the younger man called back, starting toward the canyon to intercept them, going at a jog-trot run.

"You want to reach Filmore Air Force Base—"

"I will," he told the Russian woman beside him. "We will—but we'll rest. A few hours off your feet and we should be able to move on. O'Neal can set up a defensive perimeter and stay here with the wounded."

"And Cole? He will come with us?"

"May as well," Rourke said through his teeth, his voice low, the canyon mouth looming closer now.

"I so much enjoy that man's company," she laughed, Rourke looking at her, feeling a smile cross his lips. "Why did you insist on defending me back there before the wildmen attacked—I could

8

have taken care of Cole."

"I know that," Rourke nodded.

"You are the ultimate male chauvinist, John—"

He looked at her, squinting against the sun through his dark-lensed glasses, but saying nothing. . . .

He glanced back, to his right, their bodies making long shadows across the purple-tinged ground, the sun a massive red ball on the horizon. He squinted at it, wondering. A few hours' rest had turned into an exhausted night for all, Rourke anxious to reach the base, find the six eighty-megaton warheads housed on the experimental missiles, anxious to return to the submarine that had transported them to the new west coast, then get the nuclear submarine's captain, Commander Gundersen, to take them back. He had lost now two weeks in the search for Sarah and the children. Rourke squinted at the rising sun again—how long would it continue to rise?

Natalia and Paul were silent as they walked, Paul only slightly ahead, using the Geiger counter just as a precaution. Captain Cole and his two surviving U.S. II troopers seemed to be talking to Rourke's left—but he couldn't hear the words. They wore navy issue arctic parkas, as did Natalia, only Rourke and Rubenstein wearing their own coats, the weather warmer now than it had been, all trace of snow gone. He judged the sunrise temperature at just below fifty.

They walked on.

Ahead of him, along the perfect road, no cracks in the pavement, no grass growing there yet,

Rourke could see the entrance—the main entrance—to Filmore Air Force Base. The fences were wholly intact within the limits of his peripheral vision, and the base itself seemed untouched. There were bomb craters in the far distance beyond the base, craters he could not see now, but that he had seen the previous day with the Bushnell binoculars. As he walked, he theorized the bombing technique. An Air Force Base, it would likely have been hit early—they were not bombs, of course, but ICBMs with neutron warheads. No plane would have gotten this far in the early hours of the Night of The War. That the field itself was untouched was mere chance, no missile guidance system was that precise to drop just outside the base's perimeter and thus leave the base untouched—ready to use again.

"John—" It was Natalia.

"Yeah—I see it," and Rourke looked at her for an instant, then back toward the growing definition of the base itself—a reflection from a water tower not far inside the base fence line. Glass perhaps— glass from a scope. "When I give the word—fan out—fast," he said, loud enough that Cole and his troopers would hear, loud enough that Paul would hear as well. The younger man looked back over his shoulder then, nodded, and glanced toward the field. He had seen the reflection as well, Rourke thought. "Likely a sniper up in the water tower— that's a good sign. If it isn't the wildmen, then it's likely one of Armand Teal's people—"

"Bullets are bullets," Cole snapped without looking back.

Rourke answered nothing. He kept walking, his

eyes squinted against the glare from the water tower. He was waiting for it to shift—just slightly— because the nearer they could get to the fence the better their chances would be. The sniper—if it were a sniper and he estimated that it was—would have predetermined fields of fire and ranges. There would be range markers.

As if she read his mind—he wondered if perhaps she could—Natalia rasped, "There is a small pile of rocks by the side of the road twenty yards ahead— the rocks are darker than most of the others here."

He only nodded. The sniper would attempt to hold his fire until they were near the marker. He would have used the Pythagorean Theory to calculate the range, the height of the water tower a known side of the triangle, then paced out distance to the marker, the second known leg. The third side of the triangle would simply be a basic computation then, the scope zeroed for that distance. A good man, under such fixed conditions, using a good rifle—like his own Steyr-Mannlicher SSG, he thought absently—could use an eyeball as a target and hit it. The bullet drop figures would be memorized, or more efficiently printed out and taped to the stock for instant consultation.

He wished he had the Steyr now—given its near unbelievable accuracy in a production rifle designed specifically for counter-sniper utility, and given his familiarity with the weapon, he could use the glare of the scope in the tower as his target—

"I saw it move," Natalia murmured.

"Yeah," he nodded. "So did I." He was counting to himself, trying to pace the man. If he could

11

disperse the potential targets at the precise instant before the man would shoot, that would give them more time to run and seek cover before another aimed round could be fired. Snipers, by their very nature, had to be precise.

His palms sweated.

"Take cover!" He shouted the words, pushing Natalia with his right hand, running left. There was a loud crack—a nonmilitary rifle, he decided. The glare from the scope shifted as Rourke shouted, "Throw some fire up there!"

He could hear the lighter cracks of the M-16s Natalia, Cole, and the two U.S. II troopers carried. Rubenstein wasn't shooting—there wasn't the familiar 9mm burping of the German MP-40. It was a close-range weapon.

Rourke threw himself to the dirt, the CAR-15 snapping up to his right shoulder, his legs spread wide, his left hand ripping away the scope covers, dropping them as the hand settled to the fore-end, the first finger of his right hand touching the Colt's trigger, the reticle settled on the glare of the scope. The rifle wasn't built for tack-driving accuracy at two hundred and fifty yards, nor was the scope.

He fired once, twice, a third time, then snatched up his scope covers from the dirt by the side of the road, pushed himself to his feet and started to run again, the heavy-caliber rifle from the water tower firing again.

The fence line was less than fifty yards and he ran toward it, glancing once behind him and to the right—Natalia and the others were running, firing, short bursts aimed at the general direction of the tower, to make the sniper hesitate before firing, to buy an extra second.

A rock near Rourke's right boot exploded, dust and rock chips flying up from it as the crack of the rifle came again. Rourke kept running, the fence now twenty-five yards.

He brought the CAR-15 up, pumping the trigger three more times, at once trying to draw fire toward himself and to pin down the sniper. The sniper rifle cracked again, Rourke feeling a searing pain in his left ear. "Shit!" he snarled, his stride breaking as he stumbled, but he caught his balance, kept running.

Natalia's voice— "John!"

"Okay," he shouted back, running, his breath coming hard now, the fence less than ten yards away. "Gotta go over the fence—"

"Electrified!" Cole was shouting now.

"Bullshit—not enough power—I hope!" He kept running, five yards remaining. "Cole—you and your men, keep that sniper tucked down—Paul and Natalia and I'll go over first."

"Barbed wire, John!" It was Paul.

Rourke didn't answer him, nearing the fence now, shifting his pack off to the ground, the rifle in his right hand shifting to his left so he could turn it around, the safety going on, his right hand grasping the assault rifle backwards, his left hand reaching out for the fence as he threw himself against it, his right boot finding a brace against the chain link, his right hand snapping the rifle up, the butt plate catching on the top line of barbed wire, Rourke hauling himself up, freeing the rifle, heavy assault rifle fire

13

from behind him now, the sound of bullets ricocheting off the metal of the water tower, Rourke slipping his left arm from the leather bomber jacket, grasping the rifle with his left hand, hooking the pistol grip over the wire, holding now by the butt stock.

The sharp crack of the sniper's rifle—a loud pinging sound as he glanced right—the nearest vertical support for the chain link was dimpled and bright. He freed the bomber jacket from his right arm, throwing it inside out over the wire, the heavy leather of it over the barbs. "Paul!"

The younger man shouted something Rourke couldn't hear, but he could feel the fence shaking, hear the rattling sound of the chain links against one another, Rourke throwing his weight down and to the side, further compressing the barbed wire.

Rubenstein went past him, up, over, and dropping. "Shit—"

"Natalia!"

His right hand grasped at the chain links nearest him, his grip on the CAR-15's butt stock slipping a little. He could hear the fence rattle again, the woman going past him, up, over the fence. He followed her with his eyes—she landed as gracefully as a cat after the twelve-foot drop. She was already moving, her M-16 spitting fire, Rubenstein running, limping slightly.

"Cole!"

Rourke's left arm ached—the armpit burning as his muscles screamed at him. The fence shook and rattled again, then Cole was up, past him, dropping, the man after him stopping at the top of the fence,

14

firing a burst from his M-16, more of the assault rifle fire coming from inside the compound now, but not all from Natalia and Cole. There was the lighter rattle of Rubenstein's subgun, a short burst, then another and another.

The second of the U.S. II troopers was coming, up, over the top of the fence.

Rourke threw his body weight left, his right arm reaching out, grasping at the chain links. The heavy crack of the sniper rifle, part of the chain link supporting him peeling back as the bullet sliced it.

Rourke released his grip with his right hand, throwing his hand up and out, catching again at the fence, hauling himself up, leaving the CAR-15, its sling entangled in the broken section of chain link, leaving his bomber jacket as well. He hauled himself to the top, throwing his weight over, sideways, his legs in clear air, his hands releasing their grips. He dropped, hitting the dirt hard, losing his balance, rolling.

He pushed himself up, snatching at the Detonics .45 under his left armpit and then the one under his right. He started to run. The heavy-caliber rifle discharged again, into the concrete near his feet as he hit the road again, more assault rifle fire coming from a squat bunkerlike building a hundred yards distant, another heavy-caliber sniper shot, Cole cursing, "Damn—shattered my stock." Rourke didn't bother to look. There was a sentry house fifteen yards to his right and he aimed for it, Natalia and Paul Rubenstein there already, Paul firing up into the water tower with his pistol—seventy-five yards at least and useless—and Natalia pumping

15

neat, three-round bursts from her M-16.

Rourke reached the sentry house, slamming himself against it, Natalia firing again, catching his breath. He looked at her, leaning down as he did, putting his head toward his knees.

"Are you all right—your—your ear—"

Rourke suddenly remembered it, touching at it. "Are you all right—how's your abdomen after going over that fence—"

"I can tell where your suture line from the operation was," she smiled. "But I'm all right—you're a good surgeon. Let me look at your ear—"

"No time—gotta—"

"Let me look at your ear," she ordered, stepping closer to him. "Paul!"

Rubenstein turned toward them, Rourke looking up, Natalia handing Paul her rifle.

"Try this—"

"Right," he nodded, pushing his wire-rimmed glasses back off the bridge of his nose, taking the assault rifle and leaning around the edge of the sentry house. The sniper rifle fired again, the report louder this time.

"Three fifty-seven H&H maybe," she said absently.

Rourke nodded, sucking in his breath hard as she touched at his ear. "Paul—you were limping."

"I'm fine—just gave myself a little twist—worked it out when I ran."

"Good," Rourke nodded, fighting the pain again, gritting his teeth as he felt her probe the wound.

"You should have a scar—you are very lucky.

16

Like they say in your American movies—'' her voice was soft, low—a perfect alto. "Just a crease. It really was—a lot of blood, small tear in your flesh on the upper portion of the outer ear."

"The helix," Rourke corrected.

"As a doctor, you call it the helix—as a KGB major with only some first aid training, I'll call it the upper portion of the outer ear, thank you."

"Right," Rourke groaned.

"It's bled enough, I don't think there's risk of infection—medical kit is in your pack?"

"You got it," he nodded.

"I think the bleeding is stopping—"

"Probably start up again when Paul and I head for that water tower," he told her mechanically, then raised his voice, moving away from her, toward the edge of the sentry house. "Cole?"

"Here!" The U.S. II captain's voice came from behind a truck—a two-and-one-half ton—parked just beyond the second gate, the gate swung closed now but nothing locking it as Rourke glanced down the road. "Maybe three or four guys—that low building!"

"Keep 'em pinned down—assume they've got a lot of ammo—so don't worry about burning up yours," Rourke called back.

He looked behind him to Rubenstein. "Give Natalia back the M-16—we both head through the gates, then you to the left and me to the right. Once you're inside twenty-five yards of the tower, find some cover and keep burning sticks into the tower. I'm climbing it—"

"Let me—get you bleedin' again."

"No," and Rourke turned toward Natalia. "You keep him pinned down—the sniper—keep him down while Paul and I make the run, then give Paul some fire support while I climb. We'll be okay—that scope won't help him at the distance."

"All right," she nodded, her blue eyes wide. "Be careful."

Rourke felt his face seam with a smile. "I always am," he whispered. The Detonics stainless .45s in his fists, he glanced to Rubenstein. "You ready?"

"Aww, sure," Rubenstein smiled. "Nothin' like a good running gun battle to start the day off right."

Natalia laughed. Rourke didn't. "Let's go," he rasped through his teeth.

He started to run.

He hit the gate a half-step ahead of Rubenstein, shoving against it, the gate swinging wide, Rubenstein shouting, "Race ya—I'm younger!"

Rourke laughed then, yelling, "Bullshit!" He bent into a run, his arms at his sides, his fists balled on the black checkered rubber Pachmayr grips, his feet hammering against the concrete road surface, the concussion of each step rattling through his frame, feeling the warm moisture of blood again by the upper portion of his left ear.

Rubenstein wasn't outdistancing him, but was keeping even as Rourke glanced left, the New Yorker with the high forehead pushing his glasses up on his nose again as he ran, his right hand holding the subgun tensioned on its sling away from his body. He was nearing a Jeep.

"Go for it, Paul—watch if he hits the gas tank!"

"Gotchya!"

18

Rourke kept running, his heart pounding in his chest—he felt himself smile. Rubenstein was younger—

Rourke threw himself against the timbers supporting the water tower, hearing the boom of the rifle overhead, hearing the pinging sound as a shot ricocheted off the Jeep behind which Paul had taken cover. There was the rattle of subgun fire, Rourke catching his breath, working his way around to the rear of the water tower. Assault rifle fire hammered into the timbers—from the low blockhouse.

"Cole!" Rourke shouted, not knowing if the U.S. captain could hear him. But did Cole think he really still needed him? They had reached the base—if the missiles were here—but there was still Armand Teal, Rourke's old friend, the base commander—he was still to deal with.

Assault rifle fire from the deuce and a half—the fire aimed toward him by the timbers ebbed.

Rourke upped the safety catches on both Detonics pistols, holstering them in the double Alessi rig, securing the trigger guard breaks. He started up, hand over hand, diagonally, following the pattern of the cross timbers. He laughed at himself. In high school years ago, some of his friends had dared him to climb a water tower, to spray paint the name of the local football team there before the homecoming game. He'd declined it—vandalism. But now he was doing it—instead of with a can of spray paint, with two automatic pistols, a .357 Magnum revolver and a knife.

Irony, he thought. "Irony."

He kept going, more assault rifle fire hammering

into the timbers around him, then answering fire from Cole and his men. There was fire from Natalia's position—he relied on her accuracy with his life, climbing under her line of fire to reach the parapet around the water tower where the sniper lay.

He kept going, judging the distance remaining as perhaps thirty feet. The rattle, the chatter of Rubenstein's submachine gun. The boom of the sniper rifle.

Twenty feet to go. Reaching out to a timber above him, the timber gave way, Rourke losing his balance, reaching out with his hands, finding the diagonal reaching support, his feet swinging in mid-air, then finding a purchase. He started up again.

Fifteen feet to go.

Rourke kept moving, more assault rifle fire coming at him, more answering fire, then the original fire ebbing.

Once the sniper was removed—one way or the other—he thought, they could close with the men in the blockhouse. Ten feet. Five feet.

Rourke swung under the parapet, the boom of the sniper rifle was what he was waiting for.

He heard it, could hear the bolt being speed-cocked, pushed himself up, rolling onto the parapet, squinting against the rising sun as he snatched the Python from the flap holster on his right hip, the six-inch, Metalifed and Mag-Na-Ported Colt snaking forward as the sniper turned, the muzzle of his rifle a gaping, black hole.

"John—John? Here?"

The voice. The face—worn, exhausted, oddly

smiling.

Rourke lowered the muzzle of the Python.

"Armand Teal," he almost whispered.

Without another word, Teal shouted at the top of his lungs, "Hold your fire! These are friends! Hold your fire!"

The fire from the blockhouse stopped. The sun was fully up on the horizon now. It was quiet except for the shuffling of feet on the road surface below as the blockhouse began to empty.

Chapter Two

Sarah Rourke had dug the grave, her hands aching from the rough stick she had used to claw at the ground, Michael beside her scooping handfuls of dirt away still. It was shallow, but Millie Jenkins had only been a little girl, and the earth here would be deep enough to hold her, to cover her—forever.

Sarah stared at the yawning grave—her spine tingled with what her husband John had once told her was a type of involuntary paroxysm. She called it terror.

"That's deep enough," she whispered, reaching out and touching her son's shoulder.

He looked up at her, his face and hands dirty from the dirt of the grave. More dirt as he smudged away sweat from his forehead.

"It's deep enough," she repeated slowly.

"I'm gonna kill every one of them."

She turned around when she heard the voice—it was Bill Mulliner. "No, you're not," she whispered. "You have your mother to take care of—us to help take care of."

She took her son's hand in hers, still looking at Bill Mulliner for an instant longer, then looking at

Michael's hand. The bleeding had stopped as she removed the bandana handkerchief she'd used as a bandage. "You wash your hands, Michael—it'll hurt. Use soap with the canteen water."

"You, too," he told her, smiling, his eyes not smiling, though. His right hand and her left had been wounded simultaneously as she'd held his hand, the edge of her hand, the fleshy part of his behind the thumb.

"I will," she told him. "After we bury Millie."

"I will, too, then—after we bury Millie."

She only nodded. . . .

Mary Mulliner stood alone, even though Bill was beside her. He didn't reach out to his mother. He clenched his own hands together in prayer. Annie stood beside the grave, staring down into it, at the blanket-wrapped body of the slightly older little girl—a girl Annie had played with on and off since the morning after the Night of The War. Annie looked up at her then, Sarah hearing the words the little girl—her daughter—spoke. "Will the worms eat her—will they eat Millie up? On television once they talked about this man being buried and the worms ate his—"

Sarah dropped to her knees, loosing Michael's hand, hugging the little girl to her. "Annie—don't—"

Annie cried, like she used to cry when you told her she had done something wrong, Sarah thought. "Millie isn't here now," Sarah began. "She's gone to—"

Sarah looked up. Bill Mulliner was singing.

"Amazing grace, how sweet the sound—"

24

His voice was poor, hoarse, choked sounding. Mary Mulliner began to sing as well.

"That saved a wretch like me—"

Sarah made herself join them, her own children silent, crying. "I once was lost—" she murmured. . . .

The grave was covered with rocks Annie and Michael had gathered, rocks of all sizes and colors, quartz types Sarah recognized—she had tried jewelry making once as a hobby—and others she couldn't. Bill Mulliner, an M-16 in his right hand, another slung cross-body across his back, stared away from them, at the grave, Sarah thought.

"Don't know if David Balfry got hisself away," Bill's voice came, still choked sounding. "With Pete Critchfield away and all, though—there should still be a Resistance left, leastways—we'll find him. Find a safe place for you, Mrs. Rourke—and for Mom."

"Yes, Bill," Sarah answered.

"We can find 'em" Bill Mulliner said.

Sarah said nothing—there was no choice with Soviet troops all throughout the countryside. And there was nowhere else to go, anyway. "Yes, Bill," she said again. . . .

Chapter Three

The almost cylindrical-shaped coffin emitted a blue light—a ghostly light, Colonel Nehemiah Rozhdestvenskiy thought. He stared at the cylinder, the form inside it, the myriad lights on the console attached with electrical conduit to it. He turned to the man beside him. "When will you know, Dr. Vostov?"

"You realize, colonel," the white-haired, white-coated man beside him began, removing his glasses, gesturing with his pipe, "that testing under field conditions is the only real way to evaluate—"

"You realize, Comrade Doctor, that to test under actual field conditions is totally impossible."

"This has not escaped me, Comrade Colonel." And Vostov looked away.

Rozhdestvenskiy could see his own and the doctor's reflection in the glass between them and the swirling blue lights of the coffinlike object. "Perhaps if more of the details surrounding this Eden Project affair of the Americans were made available to me—"

"You have been given, Comrade Doctor, as much of the scientific data as concerns the Eden

Project as we ourselves have—"

"Then perhaps," and he turned to face the doctor as he saw the doctor's reflected image on the glass, turning to face him, "Comrade Colonel—perhaps you have not the sufficient data yourself," and Vostov's eyebrows raised, the man replacing his glasses. "If the Americans placed such faith in this, this Eden Project, they evidently knew something which we do not, something perhaps we should know in order to achieve the success you so desire—"

"The subject was a volunteer, was he not?"

"The man in there? A volunteer given the choice of participating in the experiment or immediate execution—yes. I suppose he could be called a volunteer, Comrade Colonel."

"His life signs?"

"We do not know what to expect—of course they are not normal. I developed the serum—I have tested the serum—with only some success. Never on such a complex mechanism as the human body."

"His physical condition was perfect, was it not?" Rozhdestvenskiy asked.

Vostov smiled, removing his glasses again, sucking at his pipe, as if phrasing his answer—like a professor before a classroom of dolts, Rozhdestvenskiy thought. "No physical specimen is perfect. Even yourself, colonel. I have seen your medical records, all of the KGB Elite Corps medical records. Your weight and blood pressure and all other factors are perfect for your age, your physical size. You yourself are as close to a perfect physical specimen as one might wish to be."

Rozhdestvenskiy smiled. "But?"

"But—perfect as you are, have you never had a cold? A sudden mysterious and lingering pain, which then vanished? If we understood the human body perfectly, our task would be a simple one. If dormant cancer cells were present in the subject, for example, would the process trigger their activity? And, of course, the obvious question which has so beleagured our previous research in the Soviet scientific establishment. A living body and a dead brain are useless."

"I asked you—you have not answered me," and Rozhdestvenskiy returned his gaze to the cylinder beyond the glass, the blinking lights, the bluish haze emitting from the transparent upper portion. The cold, blue-seeming face inside. "When will you know?"

"I shall attempt to discover the answer you seek—shortly. Very shortly."

Rozhdestvenskiy sighed. "Shortly. The Womb—work here goes on apace, the weapons and supplies coming in. Should your experiment fail—"

"Then we shall not," Vostov smiled into the glass, the sucking sound of his pipe audible in the otherwise total stillness. "We shall not be able to worry, hmm?"

Rozhdestvenskiy continued to stare at the man inside the cylinder. "Live," he mentally ordered him.

Chapter Four

Teal picked up the rifle, then handed it across to Rourke. Rourke looked at it briefly. A Whitworth Express—Interarms had imported it—and the caliber was as Natalia had guessed, .375 H&H Magnum. The scope cost more than the rifle—a Kahles.

"Odd combination," Rourke smiled, setting the rifle down on the metal conference table.

"Bought the rifle—had it custom stocked—like that barrel bedding. The thing would print minute of angle at two hundred yards with an el cheapo scope on it. Figured the rifle was fine—needed a better scope. My son was in Germany—he picked up the Kahles for me when he was on a leave—that was—" And Teal stopped talking.

Rourke cleared his throat, finding one of his dark tobacco cigars, lighting it in the blue-yellow flame of his Zippo. "I, ahh—I understand a lot of our people survived over there—still fighting the Russians—maybe Fletch is still alive."

"Yeah," Teal nodded, licking his lips, looking away. "Yeah—maybe—maybe he is."

Rourke exhaled the smoke, watched it drift upward, then dissipate.

"See—ahh—we don't know much here. Like you said about this new thing—U.S. II. And Sam Chambers being President—last I knew he was filling a new Cabinet post—science and technology."

"He was the only one left."

"How is he—I mean—a—a—a good President?"

"He's got problems—he's trying his best," Rourke told him honestly.

"You sure we can trust her?" Teal asked, looking at Natalia sitting between them, then at Rourke.

"I am Russian—I don't want your people to have any more weapons. But I don't want either side to use any more. I'm his friend. You can trust me until I tell you that you can't," she answered for Rourke.

"Seems fair," Teal shrugged. "Anyway—nothin' top secret about it. See—the Night of The War, like you folks call it—well. Ever heard of EMP?"

Rourke nodded.

"ENP?" It was Rubenstein, from Rourke's left.

"EMP," Teal corrected.

"Electro Magnetic Pulse," Rourke added.

"A detonation sends shock waves through the atmosphere—the bigger the detonation and the higher up it is, the greater the shock-wave effect, roughly," Natalia said, looking past Rourke at Paul.

"Mustn't have been too big or you folks woulda known about it," Teal said, his eyes moving, shifting from Rourke and past Rubenstein toward the other side of the conference table, where Cole sat, his two troopers stationed outside the bunker with the bunker defenders. "Wiped out all our communications—destroyed the printed circuitry in all our aircraft—nothing got off the ground after the first scramble. I don't even wanna think about those guys up there—suddenly, all their electrical systems go out—no communications—they—''

Teal fell silent for a moment. "We got the communications restored after a while—scrounged up all the old vacuum tubes I could find and with Airman Raznewicz we made up a working radio. Couldn't reach too far with it though. Got several of the helicopters and a dozen fighters to where they'd work. Figured we'd at least have something our guys could use when we got help. But, ahh—'' Teal lit a cigarette. "Got plenty of these—the BX just sent a shipment in day before it—it, ahh—happened. Enough for a couple thousand guys hooked like me for a—''

"How did you survive, colonel?'' Cole asked, Rourke looking at Cole across the table, then down into his hands.

"With everybody on alert, I—ahh—I was in the command bunker here. With the intelligence people—you know?'' He puffed on the cigarette. "In the intelligence vault. We got hit—no warning at all. The senior airman on vault duty jumped for the door and slammed it shut—he was on the outside. I wrote up a commendation for him—don't know if he has a family left to know about it. He saved our lives, though. For what, I—'' Teal looked at his cigarette. "I thought—when we tried our communications—when we didn't get anybody. I thought maybe we were the last ones. All the old frequencies—dead. Lot of Soviet jamming. Didn't know—only eighteen of us survived the whole thing—most electronic intelligence guys, couple of senior officers.

"There were television security monitors inside—that was before the pulse. We watched the missiles falling—thought we were all—but then people just started dying. You could watch 'em—just dying. Sick—just, ahh—" Teal stopped, stubbing out his cigarette—a Marlboro—and taking another cigarette—a Winston. "See, I try all the different brands—so do the rest of the guys. So when one brand runs out, it won't be that—hard to take," and Teal sank his face into his hands. Rourke thought he heard a sob, covered up with a cough, then Teal looked up, his eyes wet.

"Thought maybe—well—we were the only Americans left at all—anywhere."

Rourke inhaled hard on his cigar—it had gone out. He took the Zippo and relit it.

"Couldn't bury the guys when we got out," Teal continued. "Just too many of them—thirty-four hundred and twenty-eight. Thirty-four hundred and twenty-eight. Not just guys, women, too. Some wives and kids—my wife—"

Teal stood up, his chair falling backward, slamming and echoing against the concrete floor. He walked away from the table, Rourke watching him, knowing everyone else was watching him, too.

There was nothing to say. . . .

They sat now outside the bunker, the sun strong at nearly midday, Rourke eating a Milky Way from the BX, Natalia smoking from a fresh carton of cigarettes. "This is my brand—my favorite one. I always liked your American cigarettes," she said suddenly.

"We hauled all the bodies," Teal began again suddenly. "Hauled 'em—over there," and Rourke followed with his eyes where Teal gestured—a burnt-out hangar across the field. "Took us—well—a long time. And the bodies—well. By that time—but we couldn't use a wooden structure—afraid the fire would spread. Had plenty of aircraft fuel though. So we doused all the bodies with it. One of the airmen used to live in Kentucky—worked at a fireworks factory for a while. Said he knew how to blow things up. We let him do it after I—I prayed—"

Natalia dragged hard on the cigarette—a Pall Mall.

Rubenstein visibly swallowed. "We did something like that—John and I did—we were on a plane—the Night of The War—some guys came along. We call 'em Brigands—men and women. They, ahh—"

"A massacre," Rourke finished for him. "What about your position here—I didn't see eighteen men. The wildmen? That why the sniper post?"

"Yeah—that and the Russians if we ever see 'em—guess we aren't important."

Cole laughed.

Rourke looked at him.

"Wildmen—good a name as any," Teal laughed. "See—I'm the only qualified pilot. And I couldn't leave the base—give up my command—maybe there would be something we could do, you know? So I sent out four men—just to get the lay of the land. They had decontamination suits—everything. Should have come back. But they never came back—not at all.'' Teal lit a cigarette, Rourke watching as he took another bite of the Milky Way. With a medical kit, Natalia had cleaned and bandaged his left ear. He'd taken a painkiller—a mild one—but it had somehow made him hungry.

"See," Teal continued. "We didn't have any idea about the outside world—figured the only way I could tell what to do, if there were anything to do—anything—well, we needed intelligence. Pretty much all we had left here. Intelligence men. I decided to risk three more men—if I could get volunteers. Well," and Teal threw down the cigarette, stubbing it out under the heel of his combat boot. "I got 'em," he sighed. "Only one of 'em returned. But he died right away afterward. He talked about these crazy guys—half-civilized, almost half-animal—like somethin' out of some el cheapo sci-fi movie, ya know?"

Rourke nodded, that he knew.

"Anyway—they killed their victims by burning 'em on crosses—"

"How did this man escape?" Natalia asked, putting out her cigarette against the concrete steps on which she sat, her M-16 across her knees.

"Cut to pieces with some kind of spear—least that's what he said it was. Thought he was dead and stripped him, then rolled him down a hillside. Came to—freezing, bleeding. Crawled along the bottom of the hill. He could see the crosses burning, hear the other men screaming. He was a tough guy—had the survival training course. Found a stray wildman—killed him with a rock. Took some of his clothes, used the guy's spear like a cane or a staff—he hobbled in, almost dead already." Teal paused, lighting another cigarette, looking up at Rourke standing beside him. "Fletch's age, John— just a kid. Died in my arms."

Rourke ran his tongue over his lips, nodding.

"That gave me eleven men," Teal said, his voice low. "I wasn't gonna risk anybody else. Figured to wait and see. That was three weeks ago. One of the guys—an officer. He went insane, I guess—shot himself in the mouth with a 45. Another guy— Airman Cummins. Got what we all figured was appendicitis—boy, we could have used you, John. We don't have a doctor. I tried—got the medical books out—tried. He died."

"If it ruptures and you don't know what to do— the poison spreads pretty quick," Rourke said soberly.

"Yeah—it was kinda quick—I guess. So I got nine men and myself. I got five sleeping right now, one man guarding 'em. Three others—sentry posts around the base with the best excuses for sniper rifles we could come up with. Lotta guys had personal weapons we had logged in and locked up. Picked the best we could find outa those. These aren't so good for long distance stuff," and he tapped the butt stock of the M-16 on Natalia's lap.

"We held the base though," Teal concluded, then fell silent.

"The wildmen," Natalia said, half to herself. "They must think there is still radiation here. That must be why they haven't attacked."

"But with us coming in—they'll probably figure

37

it's safe,'' Rubenstein added.

"To attack," Rourke almost whispered.

"To attack," Teal nodded.

Cole spoke then. "I came for the missiles you store here—and wildmen crazies or not, I've gotta have 'em, colonel. I've gotta."

Rourke studied Cole. For the first time—"I've gotta have 'em"—he thought Cole had spoken the truth.

Chapter Five

"Russians all over the road," Bill Mulliner whispered hoarsely, sliding down into the rocks beside her.

Sarah looked at him, saying nothing for a moment, then, "What started this?"

"Maybe the supply convoy we hit—bunch of junk. Like they was hoardin' stuff, Mrs. Rourke."

Sarah looked at him. "Like what?" she asked at last.

"Everythin'—M-16s, even old .45s. Pharmaceutical stuff. Medical gear. You name it, they had it—even golf carts."

"Golf carts?"

"Yeah—the battery-operated kind. Don't know why they'd want themselves golf carts. I used to tinker with one of 'em when I was a kid. Never could get the damn thing to run—'scuse my language, ma'am."

Sarah only nodded, looking away from Bill Mulliner and down below the rocks where the children stayed with Mary, Bill's mother. "Golf carts," she nodded, incredulous. "Guns, drugs, golf carts—that's crazy."

"Yes, ma'am—but they had themselves a ton of guys round 'em. The trucks, I mean. Big fight—we beat hell out of 'em—there I go again with my language."

"Never mind," and she smiled at him, patting his right hand with her left.

"Had 'em on the run we did—set fire to some of the trucks—carted off some stuff—then more Russians came. Helicopters—shot us all to—well. You know, ma'am."

"Mmm," she nodded, thinking.

"Maybe we can hole up here in the mountains."

"Sure," Sarah laughed. "No food except what you had on you in your pack. Some stuff I had. Enough ammunition maybe for one good ten minute fight. Two children, a sixty-two-year-old woman, you and me—I don't think so," she told him, smiling again, not knowing why she was smiling.

"There's Russians all over like flies on a horse tur—" He looked at her, shook his head at himself as he cut himself off, then looked away. "Ya hang around men all the time—no womenfolk around," he said. "Well—you know, ma'am."

"I know," she nodded. "Can't expect to sound like a saint when you're a soldier," and she hugged his shoulders with her left arm. "Ohh, Bill—I wish—"

"I wish we had about fifty people could fight —we could knock out them Russians down there on the road—steal what we need from 'em."

"But we don't," Sarah sighed. . . .

Chapter Six

Paul Rubenstein felt almost civilized again, he thought. Riding in a truck cab with someone else doing the driving wasn't exactly a taxi ride in Manhattan—although the bumpiness made for similar moments—but it was a definite improvement over walking out the distance to get Lieutenant O'Neal and the others from the shore party. There were two trucks—Rubenstein looking back in the sideview mirror through the dust cloud—and an ambulance following behind. The driver was Airman Standish—he was black, and Colonel Teal had told Rubenstein Standish was the man who had worked at the fireworks factory in Kentucky, the man who had taken on the grim task of setting fire to the corpses from the Night of The War.

"What's this Dr. Rourke fella like, Mr. Rubenstein?"

"Paul—my first name's Paul."

"Right—mine is Art. So what's he like?"

"Quiet—sometimes you get the feeling there's a lot boiling over inside him, but he never lets it get out. Self-control—that's what it is, I guess. That's what he's like."

"Some of the fellas was talkin'—you know. Sayin' this Rourke was in CIA or somethin'."

"Before The War—lot of clandestine operations in Latin America. Then after some big fiasco down there—he talks about it every once in a while. Figures he was set up by a double agent, maybe. But he got disgusted with it. Freelanced his services in survival and weapons training—all over the world, really. He wrote a bunch of books on survival, medical aspects of survival training, survival weapons use. Probably the top man in the field. Had everything goin' for him. I read a lot of his books—good writer. Not a half-bad sense of humor—shows up in his writing more than his talking."

"What the hell you guys doin' out here?" And Standish worked the two-and-one-half ton truck's transmission down, the gears grinding loudly, O'Neal and the others in the box canyon less than two hundred yards ahead.

"What are we doin' here? Looking for six missiles."

"The experimental ones?"

"Yeah—"

"They're a long way from here, fella," and Standish laughed, gesturing up toward the high rocks beyond the boundary of the valley. Rubenstein saw what he pointed at—wildmen.

Chapter Seven

Rourke sat in the cockpit of the prototyped FB-111HX, running the preflight check, Armand Teal on the access ladder beside him, coaching him. Rourke had never flown an F-111-type aircraft, he'd told Teal. "That's your targeting computer—there," Teal gestured, pointing past Rourke.

Rourke nodded. "Where are those missiles Cole wants?"

"About seventy-five miles away from here—past the wildmen, like you call 'em." Teal's voice echoed across the otherwise still hangar. "You're never gonna get 'em out with those crazies out there."

"Maybe you're right," Rourke sighed.

"They've got enough megatonnage to totally blot out a city the size of Moscow—and then some. Maybe that's what U.S. II wants 'em for."

"Never get through their particle beam defenses," Rourke noted absently, studying the fuel management panel in the control console to his left.

"Reconnaissance should tell the story, John—from what I figure and what you and the Russian woman told me—well. Those crazies are all over.

43

We're trapped here unless we get out by air—and I can't leave this base intact. Goes against everything I was taught, everything I believe. Leave it to fall into enemy hands. Never. The President could even order something like that—and I wouldn't. Only way to get those missile warheads out is by air. And that means helicoptering 'em here at least. Then put 'em aboard a B-52 and take 'em out.''

"The Soviets have to have radar systems going—they could pick off a B-52.''

"Fine—then that damn submarine. But you'll still need to use helicopters to get them out to the submarine. The Russian woman flies?''

"Yeah,'' Rourke nodded, looking at him.

"Well, there's your answer.''

"I haven't seen a helicopter anywhere on this base.''

"Three of 'em in the last hangar on the end. Army choppers—Bell OH-58A Kiowas. Had 'em flown in here just before the Night of The War. There was a joint services exercise being planned—never got all the details.''

"That hangar locked up?'' Rourke asked him.

"You're thinkin' of Cole, right? I don't trust him either. And, yeah—it's locked.''

Rourke looked back to the instrument panels. He studied the counter-measure warning lights on the upper right. "Counter-measures,'' he murmured. . . .

Rourke looked behind him, the action awkward feeling in the borrowed pilot's helmet, Natalia sitting there, one more seat in the fighter bomber empty. He heard her voice coming through the

44

headset built into the helmet. "You've been wanting to ask me something." The voice sounded odd—oddly near, yet different because of the radio link.

"I didn't know how to ask you," he told her, working the controls for the television optical unit positioned almost directly beneath where he sat, in the base of the fuselage. "I wasn't certain how I could ask this without somehow making you think I distrusted you—but I don't."

"Is Cole a Russian?"

"Yes," Rourke nodded, saying into his helmet radio. "Yes—that was the question. I think I asked it before."

"And you want to know if anything he might have said, might have done—might have jogged a memory or made me change my mind?"

"Yes."

"He isn't a Russian—I suppose he could be a clever GRU agent, but he isn't KGB—and I do not think he is Russian at all. Not working for my Uncle, or for Colonel Rozhdestvenskiy either—"

"Rozhdestvenskiy," Rourke repeated, watching the television monitor, rolling the name on his tongue. "The man who replaced—"

"Yes," she interrupted.

"Karamatsov."

"Yes."

"Then who the hell is Cole?" Rourke said, exasperated, still watching the monitor. He had the camera set to high-resolution zoom, manipulating the angle now to scan the ground thousands of feet below them. He saw movement, men—women likely,

45

as well. Wildmen. They appeared like ants. He started to bank the fighter bomber, rolling over into a dive to drop his altitude.

"I don't know who he is—not an American officer, I think. I have met many people in your American military—and if he is an officer, he doesn't act like one."

Rourke switched the television optical unit to off as he leveled out, skimming the ground now, consulting the fuel management panel cursorily, then glancing to his right and down, checking the compass control panel. "The signature on those orders," Rourke said finally. "It was Chambers's signature—I've seen it before."

"Yes—so have I."

"And I could see Chambers wanting the missiles as a bargaining tool against your people."

"Yes—so could I."

"But there's just something—"

"He would have needed Chambers's help to get the submarine," he heard her voice saying in his headset. "I mean, Commander Gundersen—he is very nice. He seems just as he should seem."

"Yes," Rourke agreed. "No—if Cole is trying to fool us, he's already fooled Gundersen at least enough to get his help."

"I sometimes get very sick of this—this War. The weather, the color of the sky—I think it all means something. And now this thing—this crazy man sent to obtain four hundred eighty megatons in thermonuclear warheads. All is madness, I think."

"You're thinking in Russian, speaking in English."

He heard her laugh then. "You know me so well—perhaps we two are the ultimate madness, John—aren't we?"

Rourke said nothing.

There was nothing he could say. Beneath them, shaking hands and arms and clubs and spears, were the wildmen—hundreds of them. He started the jet climbing as he saw assault rifles raised skyward, on the off chance a stray shot might hit something vital. As the fighter bomber left a black shadow on the ground beneath them—Rourke watching now through the television optical unit again—he saw more of the wildmen—or whoever they were.

"You talked about madness," he whispered into the radio in his helmet. But Natalia didn't answer.

Chapter Eight

Paul Rubenstein adjusted the power wattage selector, then checked the modulation indicator, Airman Stephensen sitting beside him. "You know," the airman laughed, "for a couple amateurs, we're doin' okay with this old radio."

"The U.S. II frequency for contact is easy to find—but they'll have to contact us after they pick up our signal—if they pick up our signal," Rubenstein told him, trying to fine tune the squelch control.

"Where'd you learn about radios?" Airman Stephensen asked.

"I was gut shot a while back—in the infirmary where I was there were lots of military manuals—I started reading up on radios—only thing I had to do. Then I took it easy for a while at John's Retreat—read about radios there, too—and lots of other stuff."

Rubenstein stood up from the antiquated radio set, pushing the metal folding chair back and walking across the room in the lower level of the bunker, stretching, his hands splayed against his kidneys, the small of his back aching.

"What's this Retreat thing you keep mentioning?" Stephensen asked, turning his chair around, making a scraping noise where the rubber cups on the legs of the chair rubbed against the tile on the floor. Stephensen—tall looking even when seated, carrot-haired and broad-faced—lit a cigarette with a match, flicking the match into the ashtray on the table beside the radio.

"The Retreat," and Rubenstein shrugged. "Well —John planned ahead for a war—or whatever. He was a survivalist for a long time. I guess he was a sharper reader of the times than most people—I don't know. But he's got this place in the mountains—in Georgia. Worked on it for years—comfortable, all the conveniences—must've cost him a fortune—"

"What'd Dr. Rourke do before The War—I mean? Just a doctor—like a surgeon or something?"

"No," and Rubenstein realized he was smiling. "No—he never practiced medicine. He was in the CIA—"

"Central Intelligence—"

"Yeah—but he went out of that. Got into teaching survival training, about weapons, writing books about it—I guess some of the books sold really well. He was in demand all the time. Spent every dime he could get free on the Retreat. He told me once he was always hoping his wife would be able to say, 'I told you so,' and the Retreat wouldn't prove out to be anything except an awful expensive weekend place. Told me once it was the only time in his life, the only thing he did in his life that he wanted to be proved wrong about. Guess he wasn't," Rubenstein

50

added, thinking it sounded lame.

"Yeah—well—I figure the world's gonna end."

"Yeah? Why?"

"Well," and Stephensen raised his eyebrows, smiling, then suddenly looking down into his hands, his high-pitched, midwestern-sounding voice dropping a little. "Well—God said in the Bible he'd end the earth again—but by fire, you know? And nuclear weapons—they're fire. Probably all of us'll get radiation sickness. If there's any babies born, probably be deformed and all—ya know? I think it's God punishing us for gettin' too smart, maybe. Too smart for our own good—like Adam and Eve did— you got Adam and Eve, don't ya?"

Rubenstein nodded. "Yes—Adam and Eve— Jews have Adam and Eve, too—and Noah like you were talking about with God's promise after the flood. We've got 'em."

"Then you know what I mean," Stephensen nodded, looking up at him.

"Yeah—then I know what you mean," Rubenstein nodded, going back to the radio set, turning his chair around, straddling it, then flicking the switch and staring at the transmit light. "Let's see if this sucker works," he sighed.

Rubenstein turned in the chair, hearing the door opening behind him.

Cole and his two men, the men holding M-16s, Cole holding his .45 automatic. Rubenstein stared at the muzzle of the gun, his right hand by the radio, not near enough to his body to reach the butt of the High Power in the tanker holster across his chest.

He started to speak, his right hand very slowly moving across the receiver to the frequency dial—he would need to feel three clicks right on the dial to be on Rourke's frequency. By moving his left elbow he could jam the push-to-talk button down at the base of the candlestick microphone. He did that, saying, "What do you want, captain?"

"It's what I don't want, Mr. Rubenstein—you and this guy contacting U.S. II headquarters."

Rubenstein felt one click. "Why not?"

"Might be embarrassing—they don't understand."

Two clicks—one more remaining until he reached the frequency for Rourke's fighter bomber.

"Where the hell is Colonel Teal?"

"You came back ahead of the wounded—we were waiting for them. Got 'em all—"

Rubenstein wanted to push up, out of his chair—but he kept his left elbow against the push-to-talk button at the base of the microphone—and he felt the third click.

"Where's Armand Teal—you kill him, too, Captain Cole?" He made the question to instantly brief Rourke—if he was listening. He didn't want to hear the answer himself because he knew it would be a death sentence.

Chapter Nine

"Teal's got a bump on the head and his hands tied. We lined up everybody else and shot 'em. And with Teal as a hostage, once Rourke and that Russian bitch land, they won't be able to go after us in a plane—couldn't risk killing Teal. I got the ball and I'm keepin' it now."

Rourke listened, glancing back to Natalia as he already began banking the plane to starboard, then glancing back to his instrument.

He heard Paul's voice and Natalia's voice simultaneously. "He's got Paul—"

"—can't think John'll let you get your grubby hands on those missiles."

"Doesn't bother me if he tries. Once I get to them, they don't go anywhere but up—all away." Rourke's ears rang, a loud burst of static.

Paul's voice, Rourke checking the altimeter, then glancing to his left and up at the airspeed/mach indicator. "You just—you just shot Airman Stephensen—in cold blood, damn you!"

Cole's voice then, "Cold blood, hot blood—what the fuck's the difference." Another noise that made Rourke's ears ring.

Natalia's voice. "He shot Paul!"

Static, then the sound of a door closing, then more static.

Rourke's right fist bunched on the control stick, his left fist hammering into his left thigh. He squinted into the sunlight through his visor—not the sun, but the tears welling up in his eyes making him do it.

Chapter Ten

He felt something touching at his shoulder, the voice not part of a dream at all.

"Comrade General—Comrade General!"

He opened his eyes, raising his head, his right hand stuck to a memorandum in an open file folder. He looked up. "What—it—what is it, child?"

"Comrade General," Catherine began. "You have been sleeping—it is late. You should go to bed, Comrade General."

He felt himself smile at her as he sat up fully, shaking loose the memorandum, watching as it fluttered from his hand to the floor, Catherine stooping in her overly long skirt and picking it up. "You are my secretary, Catherine—you are not my mother. Although I remember my mother having eyes like yours."

He felt himself smile again, Catherine blushing. "What time is it?"

"It is almost eight-thirty, Comrade General."

Varakov nodded to her, looking at his own watch, confirming it. "Yes—has there been any word since I—"

"Since six o'clock there has been no word, Comrade General—neither on Comrade Major Tiemer-ovna or the American Rourke, or the other American, Rubenstein.''

Varakov looked about his office without walls in the far side of the Museum of Natural History, the figures of the mastadons dominating the center of the great hall, the hall mostly in shadow now, only the yellow light on his desk and a light by the guard post just inside the brass doors leading from the outside disturbing the shadowy darkness. The mastadons—he stood, stuffing his feet into his shoes with considerable effort, walking toward them now—seemed somehow more ominous.

He could hear the click of Catherine's heels beside him, slightly behind him.

''A man tries, Catherine,'' he murmured.

''Comrade General?''

''A man tries. I have knowledge—knowledge I wished to share, to save as much of mankind as possible. Now I cannot. There is so little time left. If this Rourke can be found, and my niece still lives—then perhaps a few—''

''I do not understand, Comrade General.''

Varakov turned, smiling toward her, watching her face, the uncertainty at the corners of her mouth—her lips thin and pale, cast partially in shadow—raised slightly.

Varakov reached out to her, touching her hands, the steno pad she habitually carried falling to the floor between them, the pencil making a tiny sound as he heard it bounce on the stone floor. ''That you do not understand—count this a blessing, child.''

He closed his eyes, still holding her hands, in his mind seeing the mastadons—extinct—more vividly than ever.

Chapter Eleven

Rourke worked the right fuel shutoff handle, continuing the shutting down procedure as Natalia spoke to him. He removed his own helmet to hear her better. "What if Cole is waiting for us—what if he knew Paul had tuned the radio set to our frequency?"

Rourke flipped his last switch, then began opening the canopy. "He isn't that smart—and in case he is, I'll kill him," he rasped, his voice little over a whisper, the rush of cooler air on his face causing him to suck in his breath. He pushed the release for the safety harness, starting to climb out. "I'll kill him," he said again. . . .

Rourke reached under the armpits of his flight suit, drawing first one, then the second stainless Detonics .45, thumb cocking each pistol as they approached the first hangar, glancing to his left, Natalia beside and slightly behind him, the Metalife Custom L-Frame Smith .357s already drawn in her fists, sunlight dully glinting off the slab-sided barrels and the American eagles there. The flight suit was the smallest man's flight suit that could be found, short for her in the legs, though that was hardly noticeable with her boots, loose-fitting at the waist, yet the outline of her breasts under the upper portion of the flight suit distinct.

He turned away, concentrating on the hangar—if Cole were waiting it would either be on the field in one of the hangars or in the radio room where Paul and the other man had been shot, Rourke realized.

The hangar doors were open.

"You wait here."

"The stitches in my abdomen are fine—I don't have to run a race to shoot a gun anyway—the hell with waiting here," she told him.

Rourke looked at her, smiling. Sometimes he liked that about her—she didn't take orders well. "Suit yourself," he said noncommittally, then continued walking.

"I can go around back."

"Only three of them," he nodded. "Stick with me." Three of them—with assault rifles at the very least.

He stopped beside the hangar doors, the pistols tight in his hands—he half-wanted Cole to be waiting there, waiting for him. It would give him the excuse.

Natalia looked at him, Rourke nodding, diving through the doorway, Natalia beside him. He went into a crouch, both weapons poised at hip level.

"My God," Natalia whispered.

Rourke didn't look at her. He looked at the bodies along the far wall instead. "I thought good Communists didn't believe in God." He started walking, his eyes scanning across the concrete base of the vaulted-ceilinged metal structure—no sign of

Cole.

"If I were a good Communist, I wouldn't be here," he heard her say, hearing the sound of metal against leather, one of her guns being holstered.

He stopped, ten yards from the wall—dead men. The landing party, the survivors of Filmore Air Force base, bodies lurched over one another, the arms and legs in bizarre positions, heads cocked back, eyes wide open, glassy. The blood was on the concrete floor in small puddles, blood spattered over all the victims as well, hands covered with it. Rourke started nearer, watching the hands, the faces—for any sign of movement.

He stopped, beside the nearest edge of the pile of dead men, the bodies heaped upon one another as though those still living but shot had tried shielding their comrades with their bodies—a hand touched gently at the face of another man, the cuticles of the fingernails clotted red-brown.

"That butcher," Natalia's voice murmured.

Rourke looked at her. "Yes—butcher." He looked back at the dead men—his eyes suddenly catching something.

His left thumb hooked behind the tang of the Detonics in his left fist, upping the safety, his right thumb upping the safety of the second pistol, both pistols ramming into his leg pockets on the flight suit as he dropped to his knees in the blood. "Help me."

He shifted at the body weight of a black man— dead, eyes fixed. "Watch your stitches—"

"I will," Natalia answered.

A seaman, shot three times in the chest, then once

in the head. An airman, twice in the neck, twice in the abdomen and once in the head. "They came afterward and shot each one in the head."

"Yeah," Rourke rasped.

He moved the last body aside—at the base of the pile, one of the first shot apparently, lay Lieutenant O'Neal. His neck pumped blood. "He's alive."

Natalia was running, Rourke looking back at her. "Must be a first aid kit here!" she shouted back.

Natalia Tiemerovna walked briskly, her stitches itching her, her crotch itching her where the hair was starting to grow back after being shaven for the surgery. She wondered if Rourke had shaved her there—it was his way, not to let someone else see her, perhaps. She didn't have the nerve to ask him, she realized, smiling at her own embarrassment.

He was in the first hangar still, trying to keep Lieutenant O'Neal from bleeding to death.

She walked—an M-16 taken from the hangar in her hands, spare magazines stuffed in the pockets of her flight suit, awkward feeling as she walked. She stopped walking now—the command bunker doors were closed, and on the third level down would be the radio room. And Paul—almost certainly dead. . . .

Fluorescent lights burned in the hallway as she entered it from the stairwell, no living thing in sight. The radio room was at the far end—she had looked at the set before going airborne with Rourke. She sucked in her breath hard—she had been in a hurry, told Paul good-bye. She wished she had kissed him. Rourke was something besides a friend, beyond a friend—but Paul was her friend, a confidant, someone she admired and loved. She felt her throat tightening as she approached the doorway.

She reached her left hand to the knob, the right fist balled on the pistol grip of the M-16—her trigger finger was inside the guard. She turned the door handle, her right foot snapping out, her left hand slapping hard against the front handguard of the M-16 as she stepped through the doorway.

The lights were still on on the radio—Cole was "careless," she murmured. She started across the room, the airman on the floor, the top of his skull blown away and splattered across the far wall, clearly, undeniably dead.

She stopped beside the radio, her left hand going out, blood on her fingers as she touched the head. Her right thumb worked the selector of the M-16 to safe as she set it on the table holding the radio set, both hands touching Paul Rubenstein's head.

There was much blood. She smudged at it, watching as the eyelids fluttered.

A scalp wound. Despite the blood, she hugged his head against her chest, whispering, "Paul— thank God." Her own words startled her. . . .

O'Neal would live, the wound to his neck deep and bloody but packed now and the bleeding stopped. But he would be very weak. Rourke studied the man's face, O'Neal still not conscious, but sleeping rather than in a coma. Rourke heard the noise of the Jeep behind him, reaching to the shoulder holsters where he'd transferred the Detonics

.45s from the side pockets of his flight suit.

On his knees, he wheeled into a crouch, both pistols coming up, feeling a smile cross his lips as he aborted thumb-cocking the hammer spurs. Natalia drove the Jeep and beside her, hands rubbing his head—"Paul," Rourke whispered. That Natalia had brought his friend back alive, Rourke counted a minor miracle—but Cole was no less culpable. And Cole would die.

"Paul!" This time Rourke shouted the name, the guns suddenly awkward in his hands but no time to reholster them as he ran to meet the oncoming Jeep, Natalia cutting into a slight curve to her right, the Jeep skidding on the concrete hangar flooring with a squeal of brakes, bouncing as it stopped. She jumped from the driver's seat, Rourke handing her his pistols—nothing else to do with them—and stepping up into the Jeep to inspect Paul's wound.

Rourke had encountered something similar once before he remembered as he studied Rubenstein's wound, gingerly pulling back the bandage Natalia had improvised. "You have a hard head, Paul," Rourke told his friend, watching as Rubenstein forced a smile. "There was a case in Chicago years ago of a police officer shooting at a man who was rushing him with a broken bottle or something. Tried the standard things—calling halt, firing a warning shot. Finally he didn't have a choice. He fired, the shot went high and the man with the bottle had a high forehead. The bullet hit the man's forehead and glanced off. It was a .45. The man with the bottle got scared to death and ran and the cop probably died of a heart attack—a headshot with a

.45 not putting a man down. Same thing happened with you—bullet hit the right side of your head—back here," and he touched lightly at the wound, Rubenstein wincing. "Then it just glanced off. What they call a scalp wound in the movies."

"Shit—I—I feel like somebody—somebody hit me with a sledgehammer."

Rourke laughed, still inspecting the wound. "Two hundred thirty-grains of gilding-metal-jacketed lead traveling slow and steady isn't something you should expect to feel good. Now tell me all you can about Cole—anything that didn't get on the radio. But wait a minute." Rourke turned and looked behind him, Natalia smiling strangely. "What are you laughing at?"

"Men—you two are like brothers and you tell macho stories to one another and joke when you'd really in your hearts like to hug each other. Crazy."

Rourke swallowed hard, feeling his eyes smiling at her. "Just shut up and get that medical kit."

"Hmm," she smiled.

Rourke closed his eyes, shaking his head. . . .

"So I guess he either got Colonel Teal to tell him where the missiles were or figured he could sweat it out of him."

"You've been reading too many American detective stories, Paul," Natalia said, Rourke watching her smile. " 'Sweat it out of him'—really!"

Rourke rolled the thin, dark tobacco cigar across his teeth to the left corner of his mouth, saying, "But the fact remains, figures of speech aside, that what Paul said is a pretty accurate description of the situation."

"But this Teal—he seems tough," Natalia began, looking at Rourke, sitting between them on a long, low tool chest at the far side of the hangar. "If I had a complete drug kit and the time, I could get the information out of Teal. But this Cole—he is so inept—"

"So inept that he waited for the optimum chance to strike, got himself transported on faked or stolen orders aboard a nuclear submarine, so inept that we can't go after him or he'll kill Teal, so inept he'll wind up with control of six missiles—"

"Why the hell would somebody make missiles with such big warheads?" Paul chimed in.

"Should I tell him?" Natalia asked, not smiling at all.

Rourke only nodded.

"You see, Paul," she began, patient sounding, as though explaining to a child, Rourke thought, "you see—for a time it was thought that the larger the warhead, the greater and more formidable a weapon. This was before your country began searching for greater accuracy in delivery systems—like the MX missile, which caused so much controversy. A smaller warhead that could reach to a target with virtual pinpoint accuracy had less residual effect and greater destructive capability on hard targets than something huge and dirty. These were soft-target warheads—"

"Soft target?" Rubenstein, his eyes still pained-seeming, pain-filled, repeated.

"A soft target is a population center," Rourke said emotionlessly. "A hard target is a missile silo, a command bunker—something made to withstand everything except a virtual direct hit."

"And if Captain Cole is so knowledgeable as to be able to take control of these missiles and their eight megaton warheads—"

"Then we must assume," Rourke interrupted her, "that he knows how to fire them and already has targets in mind."

"Why are we sitting here, then?"

"He wouldn't kill Teal until he knew where the warheads were," Natalia added.

"We have to wait," Rourke answered. "Teal told me there were helicopters here, in a locked hangar. After I checked your wound and while I bandaged it, I told Natalia to take a look through the rest of the hangars."

"And one was locked—the windows were shuttered. Helicopters—OH-58A Kiowas. I checked them after I shot off the lock. The choppers had been repaired—their circuitry had been burned out during the electromagnetic pulse, but apparently Teal had repaired it. There were three machines, and two of them would start. The third was partially stripped down. Apparently Teal hadn't completed repairing it."

"So, after Cole gets what he wants out of Teal, he'll keep Teal alive just in case—just in case Teal deceived him or a special access code is needed—just for insurance, and as insurance against Natalia and me—and now you. Jeeps were missing—seventy-five miles cross country, with time out to work over Armand Teal, watching out for the wildmen to attack—sometime tonight he should be there. We go airborne after dark and look for signs of Cole and the others—then we do whatever the situation allows—"

"Or demands," Natalia interrupted.

"When we were airborne," Rourke said, standing, shifting the stump of burned-out cigar in his teeth, "we saw signs of masses of the wildmen—they're going to attack here." Rourke glanced at the black-faced Rolex on his wrist. "Probably in an hour, maybe an hour and a half. Natalia is going to preflight two of those helicopters—you stay here with Lieutenant O'Neal, Paul. I'm taking a fighter out of here—it's a three-seater. I'm going to strafe the wildmen just to let them know we're interested, kill as many of them as I can since they'll all be so conveniently assembled, then land the thing somewhere nearby with a nearly full fuel load. Fighter bomber really—an FB-111HX. Carry the three of us eventually. Our ticket out of here. Then I'll land, camouflage the plane and get Natalia to pick me up with a chopper. You and O'Neal'll be on your own for a little. She'll fly me back, we'll take both helicopters and search for Cole and the others. Natalia'll show you what to do after she preflights the choppers—so you and O'Neal—he should be awake enough to keep an eye on your back—can sabotage all the remaining aircraft on the field here—don't want those wildmen crazies getting any aircraft going. This base is a loss. When Natalia and I get back, we'll rig the ammo dump and the arsenal to blow—"

"But couldn't we use that stuff ourselves?"

"I'm taking a fighter bomber, Paul—leaving the cargo area completely open. Before I take off, Natalia and I'll load some M-16s, some .223s, maybe some grenades and explosives—some medical supplies, too. Get it all aboard the craft. Just leave room enough for our bikes if we can get 'em back off the submarine.''

"That's gotta be one hell of a big airplane," Rubenstein began, starting to try and stand—not making it, slumping back, holding his head.

"You rest for a while longer—but yeah, it is a big one. But not so big I can't land and take off again in a field if I have to. The FB-111HX should be perfect for that."

"I can still help you guys loading," Rubenstein began.

"He's right," Natalia said suddenly. "We can help him over to the plane, get him aboard and he can shift cargo—he won't have to stand for that. Except for the ammo nothing should be cased—and the eight-hundred-round ammo boxes won't be that hard to lift from a sitting or kneeling position."

"Agreed," Rourke nodded. He leaned down to Paul, starting to help the man up. He glanced—as he did—at O'Neal. "Remind me, Natalia—to check O'Neal in about twenty minutes—"

She nodded, already starting from Paul's other side to help Rourke get the younger man to his feet. . . .

Rourke climbed aboard the fighter bomber. Rubenstein was already back watching O'Neal and Natalia was already preflighting the first of the two functioning army helicopters. He glanced at the Rolex—an hour had passed, Paul stronger seeming, the moderate exercise having apparently helped him.

Throwing his dead stump of cigar out the cargo door, Rourke inspected what they had liberated. Twenty eight-hundred round metal containers of .223, twenty M-16Als, modest quantities of conventional explosives apparently used in war games —no plastique—and first aid and medical supplies. He'd also taken fifty cartons of cigarettes—for Natalia. Most of the conventional explosives had been left behind—to destroy the arsenal and the ammo dump. He had also brought Teal's sniper rifle, personal belongings—clothing, mementoes, family photos—and done this in the hope that he might somehow be able to rescue his old friend still alive. It was a faint hope, but the added gear took little space.

Rourke closed the cargo door, securing it, then starting forward—he was very tired of it all. But life had left him no choice.

He strapped himself into the pilot's seat, starting to turn on the electrical systems.

Calmly—a forced calm—he watched for the oil pressure gauges to start to rise.

Chapter Twelve

He had lastly checked the radio—Natalia would receive him, he hoped. There was a somehow louder-sounding rush as the craft went airborne, Rourke hitting the landing gear retraction switches on the small console to his left, the lowering sun hitting him full face, Rourke squinting behind the dark-tinted visor of his flying helmet. He reached further to his left, adjusting the throttle controls, then the oxygen vent airflow controls—he closed his eyes for an instant, then opened them, reaching to his right, setting the air-conditioning controls to keep the cabin slightly cooler, the systems inside his suit cooler as well—he was tired, could not afford drowsiness. He glanced to his right and forward, satisfied with the fuel quality indicator. He checked the target designate panel to his left, the combat maneuver panel directly before him, feeling the throbbing of the aircraft—imagined because a throb would mean a problem with the airframe—as his right hand gently, easily—he was still feeling the controls of the unfamiliar aircraft—clutched the control stick.

"All right," he whispered into his helmet, the

visor fogging slightly as he spoke.

The infrared seeker confirmed what visually he was beginning to detect—crosses with bonfires burning beside them, at the edge of the valley surrounding the base as he swept over at mach point five. He rolled the plane into a steep right bank, pulling up and climbing, arming his weapons systems—Sidewinder missiles and the gun. Leveling out, he switched the seeker system from infrared to television, setting his weapons-control panel off computer and to manual—it was somehow something that would be more personal when done himself, by hand.

He kept his speed down, cutting off his climb, leveling out, then starting to dive, the television camera below him in the fuselage behind the nose on maximum resolution, picking up what appeared to be at least a thousand of the wildmen, perhaps more, massing. There were sticks in their hands—sticks, but at the distance only. They would, close up, be spears, assault rifles—whatever other weapon the wildmen could find and use.

By feel—he had taught himself that—he released the arming safety switch—ready.

He had flown an open bi-wing once—he imagined now the feel of the rush of wind, wind at this speed that would have ripped and torn at his flesh, cold that would have killed. But the freedom of it. Soaring out of the skies, away from the troubled land. In the far distant east as he swept down toward the valley he could see a purpleness that would be twilight. The sweep of horizon suddenly, profoundly, amazed him—the curvature.

He was reaching down to the earth, penetrating it—with death. He smiled to himself—in his old age—his mid-thirties—he was becoming a poet.

"Go—" his voice was quiet, low, whispered, addressed to the wildmen as his finger poised over the Sidewinder launch button, the steam from his breath fogging his visor again, "to—" the aircraft of which he was a part, which cocooned him, leveled—"hell!"

He worked the button.

There was a rush, a roar, a buzzing sound and a contrail of smoke, the Sidewinder from portside at the fuselage rear firing, tracking into the crowd of insane nonhumans.

Rourke pulled up the nose, the explosion belching white smoke beneath him. He started the craft to climb, leveling off then and banking into a roll, hearing some of the cargo slightly shift but not move, leveling out, arming the next missile—he started down.

They were running—he could not see faces, and it was just as well, he thought. Their faces were meaningless, an abnegation of sanity, of the thousands of years of civilization that had raised man to a point where he was capable of self-destruction.

He fired the second Sidewinder, rolling the plane, three hundred sixty degrees, almost saluting them on the ground, climbing, arcing back and rolling over, his stomach feeling it, his back aching near his kidneys, the plane leveling off, his machine gun armed, his right hand squeezing against the joystick, working the machine gun's trigger as he swept the valley. The bullets seemed to explode upward from the dirt, men and women running, falling—lost to him as he skimmed the ground low.

He set the lock, disarming his weapons systems as he climbed, another rollover, then leveled off.

He exhaled hard, the helmet visor fogging again. Mentally, Rourke calculated the casualties to the wildmen on the ground—two-thirds losses, minimum. Fuel, his two remaining Sidewinder missiles—all needed to be conserved to get himself, Natalia, and Paul—to get them home. To the Retreat, to find Sarah and the children.

He could allow it for an instant. He closed his eyes, inhaling deeply. He opened them and the television monitor for the seeker unit no longer showed the wildmen—gone.

Chapter Thirteen

Nehemiah Rozhdestvenskiy walked, cold slightly in the mountain chill, alone now.

He had never faced death before. There had been danger, sometimes mortal peril. But never certain death. Times locked in combat with superior enemies, times in dangerous lands with men and women he did not trust—but never such a certainty.

He looked skyward, feeling his jaw set. "No!"

He screamed it, hearing it echo in the hills and gorges, in the mountains, on the chill air.

The volunteer—the man inside the coffinlike machine with the blue cloud of swirling gas and light. He had done worse than to die. His body lived. His mind did not.

The Americans had the answer—it was a foregone conclusion they had possessed it on the Night of The War. Otherwise, what they had done would have been not even a gesture of fatalism. Karamatsov, his friend—he had known the Americans had the answer. He had searched for it.

Rozhdestvenskiy stopped walking, standing overlooking a valley, not seeing the mountain beside him that was to be the Womb.

One ingredient was lacking—the vital ingredient.

He had taught himself to live—without the company of a woman to love, but rather with many women. Without the security of a position where responsibility was not demanded—but rather one of ultimate responsibility. He had labored.

He stared at Heaven. If God was there, Rozhdestvenskiy now wanted Him to hear. "I will not die!"

Chapter Fourteen

"That's Rourke—or Major Tiemerovna, Cole—only ones who could fly—and they'll be after you."

Cole turned to face Armand Teal, backhanding him across the nose and mouth, blood spurting from beneath Cole's knuckles as Teal's upper lip cracked and the nose broke.

"You fuckin' bastard," Teal snarled, his words sounding thick, mispronounced.

Cole laughed. "Yeah—well, colonel—you tell me what I want to know or you'll learn what a bastard I can really be."

Cole watched Teal struggling against the military issue handcuffs on his wrists, locking his wrists behind him around the trunk of the pine tree. Cole heard an insect buzz, swatted at it and looked over his left shoulder to find the source of the annoyance.

He heard Teal laugh. Loud.

"Maybe I'm not gonna get out of this—but neither are you, captain—"

Cole didn't turn his head, still staring, saying, trying to control the tension he could feel, he could hear in his voice—"Armitage—shut up the colonel there—ram your fist into his mouth if you gotta."

Cole didn't look back, facing the rise behind them.

Wildmen, standing almost shoulder to shoulder. Mentally, he began counting them—he stopped when he reached fifty, estimating the remaining numbers combined with these to equal at least two hundred.

As he watched, the sun low, the insect still buzzing him but not daring to move his hands lest it provoke the wildmen into attack, he saw a cross, then another and another and another—four in all. They were being erected on the rise.

He heard Teal laugh, realized he was losing his control, wheeled and rammed the butt of the M-16 he held into Teal's abdomen, Teal doubling forward against the tension of his arms, stumbling to his knees, his face white, vomit spurting through his cracked, bleeding lips.

Captain Cole turned away, staring toward the rise, a bonfire being lit, a chant beginning—strange sounding—deadly sounding. He felt a chill, a paroxysm race along his spine.

Cole licked his lips. "I wish to speak with your leader—"

"Take me to your leader—bullshit." It was Teal's voice, laughter tinging it, as well as pain.

Cole began again, shouting louder this time. "I want to see your leader. I can offer him power—immense power. More than he's ever dreamed of. Nuclear power—the power of life and death—power!"

The bonfire began to crackle, audibly, as he heard his voice echo back. No one answered, no one called back to him from the rise. But there was no attack. The sun setting, he stood watching, hearing the light breeze, the moans of Armand Teal as pain began to take over bravado, and the buzz of the insect.

His palms sweated as he held his M-16.

Chapter Fifteen

The camouflage nets had been difficult to get into place on his own, but as he stepped back now from the aircraft, he was satisfied. If any of the wildmen or anyone else approached to within twenty-five yards of the craft—in daylight—it would be noticeable. But from the air, or from a greater distance than twenty-five yards on the ground, it would never have been seen. The small hand axe in the pilot's survival kit had been adequate but arduous in chopping away saplings and large branches. Leaves, dead grass—he had heaped it artistically in place.

He found himself smiling—"artistically." His wife—she was an artist—a good one, her childrens' book illustrations were prize-winning. He wondered if she still lived, if the children lived.

When the business with Cole was done—he froze, hearing the sound of helicopter rotors slicing the air, the thrumming growing louder as he turned. An army helicopter—it would be Natalia, answering the radio signal. His flight suit and helmet packed aboard the plane as were the flight suits and helmets for Natalia and for Paul, he reached to the ground, snatching up his brown leather bomber jacket—a few added scrapes and scratches in the leather from crossing the barbed wire fence when he'd first reached Filmore Air Force base, but no rips or tears. He shrugged into it, grabbing up the flap holster with his Python and the CAR-15. Not bothering to buckle the holster to his waist, he started to run further into the clearing. The draft from the helicopter's rotor blades could disrupt his camouflage job—he couldn't let that happen. . . .

Rourke opened his eyes, shaking his head, looking at Natalia at the controls of the helicopter, saying into his headset microphone, "How long have I been asleep?"

"About twenty minutes, John—have you ever listened to a man snore to you through a headset radio?"

He laughed, saying, "As a matter of fact, I have—sorry."

"We'll be touching down in about ten minutes—I have some good news for you. If I'd told you earlier, you wouldn't have slept—you'd have been too busy planning."

"What's the good news?" he asked, stretching, trying to get comfortable in the seat. "The Soviet Union surrendered?"

"I would hardly call that good news, John."

"Sorry—couldn't pass it up."

"We do still have our ideological differences, don't we?"

"They seem to matter less and less, though."

She looked at him and he watched her smile, her eyes in the small dome light and the dull green light of the instrument panel gauges looking so deep a

82

blue that he wanted in that instant to drown in them. "That's right," she smiled. "They do matter less and less."

"So—what's the good news?" he said, cutting her off.

"I used my skills and saved us a great deal of time—I decoded some dispatches from the security vault safe. They alluded to periodic maintenance for the missile silos and then I backtracked to earlier dispatches, and then I found the coordinates."

"You've been busy."

"Colonel Teal had apparently preflighted these before—after repairing them. It was easier than I'd thought it would be. And Paul, I discovered, has a natural talent for sabotage. I showed him how to set explosives for the ammo dump and the armory as well—and you should see the very neat way he crosswired the master generator control panels and landing gear panels in those aircraft. We could have used him in the KGB."

"Wonderful—wonderful for him," Rourke nodded, laughing. He couldn't quite see Paul in the KGB—nor Natalia, either, as he considered it.

"By the time we get on the ground, Paul should be through. Sabotaging was something I took a course in," she laughed.

Rourke looked at her—he said nothing. And he loved her. . . .

Chapter Sixteen

O'Neal moved slowly, weakly, Rourke doing what he felt to be the logical thing—leave Paul with O'Neal, using the disadvantage of Paul's head injury, headache still bothering him, as an advantage to shepherd the submarine officer.

Natalia beside him now, the bomber jacket zipped against the cold of the evening, his right fist holding the CAR-15 by the pistol grip, Rourke started toward the bunker.

"There would have been a crew here—wouldn't there?" Natalia almost whispered.

Rourke didn't look at her, peering into the darkness as he walked. "No—these missiles were off line as far as I could tell—which is why they're still here and not in a billion pieces somewhere inside the Soviet Union. Cover the right."

"Yes," he heard her answer.

He heard her feet stop on the dirt and rocks across which they walked. Now he looked at her, looking at him. "You realize—I worked with Vladmir in an attempt to steal the plans for these missiles once. We learned something about them, John. The warheads cannot be dismounted from the missile bodies without totally disarming the warheads—totally. Do you know how complicated that is?"

"When I was in Latin America," he rasped. "I controlled an agent who was smuggling information on Soviet missiles out of Cuba—I know."

In the moonlight—there was always moonlight when it wasn't needed, wasn't wanted—he saw her eyes sparkle, her mouth upcurve with laughter.

He smiled at her, then turned away, walking—slowly, steadily, toward the bunker.

Rourke glanced behind him once—Paul with the Schmeisser and O'Neal carrying his .45 Government Model—were bringing up the rear.

Rourke stopped at the steel door of the bunker.

Natalia's voice: "There should be a conventional locking arrangement, then a second door inside with a double combination lock."

"Can you work the combinations—I did poorly at that in spy school."

She laughed. "On the other hand, I was very good at it—a woman has a naturally more sensitive touch—I can, but it would take perhaps a few hours without mechanical assistance—I don't think the stethoscope from your medical kit would help a great deal with the types of doors they have."

"You're well-informed," Rourke told her.

"Yes," she called back.

"Yes," he murmured, mimicking her. He turned around, shouting, "Paul—if these locks will keep us out, they'll keep anyone else out except Cole—or Teal. You and Lieutenant O'Neal—I want you—"

"John!" Natalia screamed, Rourke wheeling, from the top of the bunker where it was partially

86

mounded over with earth, one of the wildmen lunging for him, a double-headed axe, the handle cut to hand-axe size.

Rourke took a half-step back, hearing the shots from Natalia's M-16, the wildman spinning out in midair, crashing down, Rourke starting to raise his CAR-15, something hammering at him from behind. He stumbled forward under its weight, the Car-15 falling from his shoulder. He twisted his face right, jerking his head left, a Bowie pattern knife—long-bladed, cheap looking but deadly enough, he decided—hammering, stabbing, biting into the ground beside his face. Rourke jabbed his right elbow, the arm already extended, back, the elbow connecting with something solid, Rourke feeling the weight sag from his back, rolling, snatching the Detonics .45 from under his left armpit, jacking back the hammer, firing at the face three feet away from his hand. The wildman's head exploded, blood spattering upward. Rourke pushed himself back, up, getting to his feet from a crouch, wheeling, still crouched, pumping the trigger of the Detonics .45 simultaneously with hearing a burst from Natalia's M-16 and Rubenstein's Schmeisser, the wildman running from the top of the mound twitching, twisting, falling, tumbling to the ground. Rourke started to reach down for his fallen Colt assault rifle.

Another burst of gunfire from the M-16, a long ragged burst from the German MP-40.

Rourke wheeled toward the sound of the subgun, wildmen rushing toward Paul and O'Neal. Rourke extended his right hand, his fist balled tight on

87

the Pachmayr gripped butt of the Detonics. He squeezed the trigger once, then once again, two of the wildmen going down, one of them at least— clutching at his throat—dead.

Rourke started to look back toward Natalia, something hammering at him as he did.

A wildman, the man nearly twice his size, he judged as they hit the ground, Rourke's right fist opening involuntarily as his elbow smacked against a small rock. The feeling in his right hand—it was gone for an instant.

His left hand hammered up, finding the fleshy gut of the man on top of him. Nothing happened as Rourke hammered his fist in hard.

On his back, Rourke snapped his left knee up, hammering it against bone, then snapping it up again, feeling the squish of testicles, hearing the scream of pain, feeling the rush of air from the man's lungs against his face, the breath foul-smelling. The man had the beginnings of diabetes, Rourke diagnosed, hammering his knee up again, another scream and another rush of the fetid-smelling breath. Rourke rolled half-right, jabbing his left elbow back into the side of the wildman's face.

He could see Natalia, the M-16 on the ground, two of the wildmen backing her against the bunker, her pistols in her hands. "Look out—Natalia!"

She started to turn, a wildman from the mound on top of the bunker jumping for her, one of the men nearest to her reaching for her, both pistols discharging, the body falling against her.

He lost sight of her for a moment as he tried crawling from underneath the screaming man half-covering his chest. Then Rourke saw her, the pistols gone from her hands, her left hand brushing a thick lock of her almost black hair back from her forehead, in her right hand the Bali-Song knife flashing open, her body seeming to form itself, shape itself into a duelist's stance, the knife flashing out hard, coming back, then stabbing outward again, snapping back, one of the two wildmen she still fought screaming and toppling forward across the man ·she'd shot.

The still standing wildman had a machete—he was advancing toward her.

Rourke crawled—the hands of the wildman on top of him still clawing at him, the feeling coming back into Rourke's right hand, his left arm pinned under the wildman, his right hip with the Python under him, the holster slipped back on the belt and too far behind him for him to reach.

The first Detonics—two shots should still remain, he told himself.

Another burst of subgun fire—Paul and O'Neal, a burst of gunfire from an M-16 as well, a scream of pain, a curse.

The Detonics was inches only from the tips of Rourke's fingers as he clawed the ground, feeling the wildman on top of him digging his teeth into his thigh. Rourke moved his left hand—slightly. He couldn't get it free to reach for the Detonics under his right arm. He started to grab for the handle of the Sting IA black chrome.

He clawed outward with his right hand—the Detonics was too far.

He twisted his right hand back, trying to get it under his bomber jacket to the second Detonics under his right arm, his left unable to reach it. But his left hand had the handle of the Sting IA. He wrenched it free of the leather, ramming it back, feeling it drag as it bit flesh, hearing the scream, the pressure of the teeth on his left thigh easing, his right fist closing on the butt of the Detonics under his right armpit, tearing at the holster to break the gun free of the trigger guard break.

He heard it, felt it, the snap opening. He pulled the second Detonics out, thumbed back the hammer and jabbed the muzzle around toward the head of the wildman, the muzzle less than two inches from the head. He averted his eyes—blood would spray, and so would razor-sharp bone fragments—and pulled the trigger once, then once again, the body rocking over him.

The man had to weigh close to four hundred pounds, Rourke figured, the head split wide and all but dissolved at the rear of the skull, but the body—in death—still pinned him.

He twisted his left hand free, shoving at the chest, then moved his right hand against the wildman's left shoulder, the muzzle of the Detonics nearly flush against it. He pumped the trigger twice, fast, his wrist aching with the pressure, the body lurching over him, his left hand pushing up against it, the body rolling clear.

Rourke staggered up to his feet, reaching for the first Detonics.

The wildman with the machete was making a lunge for Natalia, her Bali-Song flashing out and catching the glint of moonlight, the machete dropping from the man's right hand as did two of the fingers.

But a revolver was coming up in the left hand.

Both pistols in Rourke's fist, he fired, the pistol in his left hand—the first gun—barking twice, the one in his right barking two times as well, the slides locking back, the pistols empty, the wildman with the revolver in his left hand and blood gushing from the severed fingers of his right falling back, sprawling onto the ground.

Rourke wheeled, buttoning out the magazines in his pistols and letting them drop, ramming the pistol from his left hand into his belt, snatching at a fresh magazine then with his left hand, driving it up the beveled well of the stainless .45, his right thumb dropping the slide stop, the gun leaving his hand, sailing cross-body into his left, his right moving down for the Metalifed and Mag-Na-Ported Colt Python .357 at his hip. His fingers closed over the butt as he popped away the flap, his hand rolling the gun over and around on his trigger finger as he broke it from the leather. He wheeled half-right. "Natalia!"

He set the pistol sailing across the air space separating them, the woman making the Bali-Song slide from her right to her left hand, catching the Python in midair, her fist grasping around the cylinder, then the gun seeming to fly up, spin, settling into her right fist. She half-turned, the Python's six-inch barrel snaking forward, dully gleaming in the moonlight, a tongue of orange fire licking from the muzzle, another wildman rushing her, dropping.

Rourke turned, starting to run toward Rubenstein

and O'Neal, the two men pinned down by gunfire coming from the rocks above.

Rourke dove toward the shelter of a rock outcropping, snapping off two shots into the rocks. He heard the boom of the Python again, then silence, then suddenly the crack of three-shot bursts from an M-16.

He looked behind him as he reloaded his second pistol. Natalia—an M-16 spitting fire in her hands— was running toward him.

Rourke thumbed down the slide stop of the pistol in his left hand, sliding his thumb back around the tang, gripping the pistol, then pumping a fast two-round semiautomatic burst up into the rocks.

He still couldn't see Rubenstein and O'Neal, both men pinned by a heavy concentration of assault rifle fire. He heard Natalia's M-16 again, then her voice, breathless, beside him.

"How many do you think?"

"Two or three or they would have made a rush— remember, they're crazies."

"Here," and she stuffed the Python back into the flap holster on his right hip. He heard the snap of the flap closing shut. "Two rounds left in it if you started with a full six."

"Yeah," he nodded, realizing that he too was breathless.

"There could be more of them in the valley, going for the helicopter."

"To destroy it—yeah," he nodded, watching her face for an instant in the moonlight, in the instant forgetting where he was, what he was doing—she was incredibly, unreally beautiful, he thought.

Another burst of assault rifle fire from the rocks.

"Gotta nail those suckers," he rasped, finding one of his thin, dark tobacco cigars, biting off the end and clamping it between his teeth.

"I've never seen you do that before."

"Usually trim the ends with a knife at the beginning of the day," he told her. "You keep 'em pinned down—don't try getting over in the rocks to Paul and O'Neal—I'll get up there after those suckers." He reached his left hand to his musette bag, reaching inside, removing four AR-15 thirties. "Here," and he looked at her for an instant as he handed her the magazines.

"I love you, too," she smiled.

"Shut up," he whispered, leaning across in the rocks, kissing her forehead.

Rourke pushed himself to his feet, starting to run—there were three men still to kill, he judged.

Chapter Seventeen

Rourke worked his way through the rocks, the partially spent magazines in the twin stainless Detonics pistols replaced with full ones, giving him seven rounds now in each gun, the full magazine plus the round chambered. He had emptied the Python of the two remaining rounds, worked one of the Safariland speedloaders against the ejector star and loaded six into the cylinder, the Python nestled in the flap holster on his right hip.

There were sporadic bursts of gunfire from the rocks, poorly controlled bursts that ate up large quantities of ammo and had little effect on a target except by accident.

There were occasional bursts from the rocks below as well—Natalia's M-16, three-round bursts which made sparks as they hit the rocks pinning down the wildmen. Bursts from Rubenstein's subgun too, neat bursts—two or three rounds each, long bursts—accurate but too long—from O'Neal.

Rourke kept moving, seeing the three wildmen clearly now.

There was no other way for it.

He holstered the cocked and locked Detonics pistols and secured the guns in the leather, working the trigger guard breaks closed with the thumb and first finger of the opposite hand.

He reached to the Python.

He carried it for one reason only—long-range accuracy.

There were no custom parts in the gun—with some fitting he had taught himself to do, he could replace anything. It was one of the very few out of the box revolvers which could be used perfectly well without action tuning. The action was sometimes criticized as being too sensitive, too prone to fouling with dirt or debris. He had never found it so. And the strength of construction made it perhaps the most solid of .357 Magnum double actions.

He thumbed back the hammer as he extended the pistol in both clenched fists, resting his forearms on the rock in front of him but not the gun itself.

He sighted on the furthest of the three heads, then barely touched the trigger, launching the 158-grain semijacketed soft point load, the gun barely moving in his hands, his right thumb cocking back the hammer, the other two wildmen starting to turn.

Rourke fired again, taking out the man to his left, the man's face seeming to disintegrate in the moonlight.

The third man, the last of the wildmen there, was raising the muzzle of the assault rifle.

No time for a single action shot, Rourke double-actioned the smooth trigger. The third headshot made, he waited quietly in the rocks—just in case there were others of the wildmen he had not detected.

He had a Python in storage for his son—one of the newer, stainless steel Pythons. He had a Detonics stainless for him as well. He wondered if he would ever see Michael Rourke again.

"John—are you all right?"

It was Natalia—John Rourke took what he judged a full five seconds before answering her.

Chapter Eighteen

Lieutenant O'Neal had originally been a missile officer—before the complement of missiles from Commander Gundersen's nuclear submarine had been fired out on the Night of The War. His "unemployment" was the cause of his being with the shore party to begin with, and of his eventual sole survival despite his wounding.

Rourke thought of that as O'Neal, still weak but seemingly invigorated from the fighting, waxed eloquent over their predicament. "She's right—Major Tiemerovna, that is. What she described from the homework she did on this system—assuming all her facts were straight—"

"We had a very highly placed source," Natalia smiled. "But he's dead now anyway—I think."

"Yes—but assuming everything he gave you about the missiles was true, you're right, major. Disarming these would be very tricky—impossible once they were armed. You always get intelligence stuff on a need to know basis, but you pick things up, things you aren't supposed to know. This irretrievable system—The No-Recall was what they called it. Once they were armed, the only thing you could do was fire them."

Rubenstein, leaning against the steel doors of the bunker, pushed himself away from the doors, saying, "That's stupid!"

"Yeah—a lot of us thought so, Mr. Rubenstein," O'Neal nodded, shifting his position on the ground, obviously uncomfortable. "Nobody asked us, though. It was—" and O'Neal looked up at Natalia, standing opposite him, beside Rourke. "I ahh—it was to guard against Soviet sabotage of our missile systems—"

"Don't apologize to me—I'm still an enemy agent," she told him, her voice a warm alto, contrasting sharply, Rourke thought, with her words.

"Well, then—what'll we do—"

Rourke looked at Paul. "You and O'Neal hold the position—against Cole. Three of them, two of you—shouldn't be that difficult. Natalia and I fly back to the submarine with the two helicopters—bring back reinforcements. Shouldn't be more than two hours—three tops. Those wildmen we killed were foragers, I guess. Either that or something like a patrol. These doors are bombproof, so they weren't trying to get into the bunker—you can see from these scorch marks where somebody tried it—likely some of these guys, and they learned they couldn't. If I'm wrong and there's a big concentration of wildmen coming, get out—we'll pick you up—fire a flare from that H-K flare pistol of mine—"

"There are flare guns in the helicopters—"

Rourke glanced at Natalia. "Better still. So, either way," Rourke said, taking his rifle from where it leaned against the bunker doors, "it shouldn't be rough duty. Stay up in those rocks—Cole comes, keep him away from the bunker. The wildmen come, beat it out of here—and they'll keep Cole away. Then we can try to do something about getting inside—that may be where you come in," Rourke said, looking at Natalia.

She laughed.

"What's so funny, major?" O'Neal asked, his face wearing a strange expression.

"A KGB major being aided in breaking into an air force missile bunker by the United States Navy—"

Rubenstein said it. "She's right—that's funny—"

Chapter Nineteen

Cole's palms still sweated on the M-16 he held, the bonfires glowing now, the wildmen unmoved since they had first encircled him, his two men and his prisoner.

"Armitage," he called.

"Yeah, captain—"

"If anything happens—shoot Colonel Teal in the head—a coupla times—"

"Yes, sir," Armitage nodded.

Cole looked at the man—the casual way he had answered. He had known Armitage for three years. They had trained together in Alabama at the camp there. They had played the war games together, listened to the speeches together. He had been with Armitage the time they had fire bombed the car of the black television reporter.

Cole studied the flaming cross—it amused him. That he should be intimidated by a flaming cross.

"Armitage," he called out.

"Yeah, captain?"

"You and Kelsoe—get ya some tree limbs—make us a cross, too—you remember how?"

Armitage said nothing for a moment, Cole watching him, then watching as the face lit with a smile, the firelight of the bonfire surrounding them, making his face glow red, almost diabolical looking.

"And light it, Captain?"

"Yeah—and light it, Armitage."

"Yes, sir!"

Cole watched as Armitage ran over to Kelsoe, Kelsoe producing a hand axe from his belt.

"Show you bastards how it's done," Cole murmured, looking again at the wildmen.

Chapter Twenty

Sarah Rourke walked through the darkness, Bill Mulliner opposite her and slightly ahead on her right, Michael walking with Annie and Bill's mother, Mary Mulliner. Michael would alert her, she knew, so she concentrated her attention, focused her senses ahead of them—there had been noises, telltale noises only. There were people at the base of the funnellike defile. But there were Russian troops on the road and staying on the high ground would have meant capture. For this reason only, Bill—Sarah realizing she had coached him—had decided to lead them down into the defile.

Brigands possibly, or more Russians—but possibly more Resistance. They were gambling.

She had come to understand herself more as a woman, she thought, trying to force her attention away from her thoughts and to the task at hand—but unable to.

She had come to understand what she could do—the power she had. Bill—a boy really, little older than Michael—was a man. He was the natural leader. But she had weathered more combat than he had, endured more, had a greater depth of judgment and perception than his years allowed him. She knew that—he knew that.

So she advised rather than attempting to lead, implied rather than ordered.

The same result was achieved—yet Bill had his self-respect as a man.

She considered herself lucky to be a woman—there were fewer problems with ego where practical matters were concerned. She was content to respectfully follow his orders—so long as they were orders that followed her own directives, however subtly given.

She understood too some of the things that had caused the tension in her relationship with her husband. He would not be implied to, be coached, be nudged along. He had never once refused to listen to a direct suggestion, an idea. But he had refused oblique direction—and it was unconscious with him, she thought.

They were incompatible—had always been. But had always loved each other.

They stopped as they reached the base of the defile. Sarah Rourke wondered if she would ever see John Rourke again, ever feel his hands on her skin—ever argue with him again.

"Bill—" she almost hissed the name, keeping her voice low.

"This way," he nodded.

She realized suddenly she had been pointing the muzzle of her rifle in the same direction he had picked—had he read it, realized she had wanted them to go that way because the ground was more even-seeming in the starlight and would be easier to traverse at a dead run if necessary?

She shuddered slightly—power.

Chapter Twenty-One

They had walked along the natural path in the woods for more than a half-hour, she judged, glancing at the watch carried in her jeans pocket. She would have to improvise a band for the Tudor so she could wear it on her wrist. That could come later, she thought—if there were one, a later.

For the last two minutes she had heard the telltale noises again. She had left Michael and Annie with Mary Mulliner, being practical and giving Michael her M-16—Mary was the worst shot Sarah had ever seen. She laughed at herself—before the Night of The War, she herself was the worst shot she had ever seen, would never have touched a gun except to move it out of the way when she dusted the house, would never have left her young son with a loaded gun in his hands.

The Trapper .45 felt good in her hand, her right fist clenched around it. She carried it cocked, her right thumb poised over the locked safety. She ducked under a low-hanging tree branch, the branch snagging at the blue and white bandana handkerchief covering her hair.

"Shit," she murmured. Bill turned, looking back

at her, and she shook her head to signify nothing was wrong. Saying a word like that—she would rarely if ever have said it before the Night of The War. It was the people she had associated with since then, she thought—they swore sometimes. And now she did, too.

She kept moving, watching Bill Mulliner as much as she watched the trail and the shadows beyond it where the meager starlight didn't penetrate.

Sarah heard something—she wheeled, something hammering at her, driving her down.

Her thumb depressed the upped safety, the muzzle of the .45 searching a target as though it had become independent of conscious thought.

She found flesh, the pistol rammed against it, her first finger touching at the trigger.

"Sarah!"

The voice was low, a whisper, whiskey-tinged. The breath smelled of cheap cigars—

"Sarah—it's me—"

She edged her trigger finger out of the guard, finding the safety before she moved anymore. She sank her head against the man's chest. She had never thought she'd be so happy to see the Resistance leader, Pete Critchfield.

"Pete." She said the name once and quietly—he was more competent than she. She needed that now.

Chapter Twenty-Two

The wood crackled as the cross burned and Cole felt somehow safer—He watched the wildmen, watching him now, puzzled that he too had ordered a cross erected, but only to burn it.

"When the hell somethin' gonna happen, captain?" It was Kelsoe, crouched beside him, Armitage sitting on the ground near where Teal was handcuffed to the pine tree.

"Soon, Kelsoe—real soon."

"Soon—they're gonna come down here and cut us up into little pieces, captain."

"Maybe," Cole nodded—he looked up at the wildmen on the ridge. "If they haven't yet—well, maybe they are gettin'—"

"Cole—"

It was Armand Teal. Cole turned, facing him, shifting his position on the ground, his legs stiff from squatting beside the burning cross. "Yes, colonel?"

"What the hell you plan to offer those lunatics—power. What power?"

Cole stood up, his legs unable to take it anymore, cramping. "Well—I guess you could call it the ultimate power. The power of the sun. The power to destroy—''

"You're gonna give them a goddamn missile?"

Cole shrugged and turned away. There was movement now on the rise, the lines of gaping wildmen separating, forming almost a wedge as Cole watched, a new group of wildmen coming from the center of the wedge—they seemed better armed as best he could judge in the firelight and the light from the torches they carried.

"Throw down your weapons!" It was a voice, loud, powerful-sounding, coming from the opening in the wedge.

"No," Cole shouted back. "I come to offer you power—not to surrender myself and be killed!" He was gambling—he knew it.

"Throw down your weapons!" The voice sounded again, as if whoever spoke had not heard him.

"The ultimate power is what I offer—power undreamed of for your leader!"

A man stepped forward then. He held no torch. He held no rifle. What looked like a fur pelt—at the distance Cole could not tell if it was the skin of a dog or a bear—was draped around his shoulders. He seemed short, or perhaps only by comparison to the well-armed men with torches who flanked him. His body seemed thick—but it could have been the animal skin he wore like a robe.

The voice was not the one that had called for Cole to lay down his weapons.

It was higher-pitched, almost amused-sounding.

"An audacious man—there are hundreds of us.

112

Four of you and one is apparently your prisoner. You offer me power—undreamed of, ultimate power? I like a sense of humor. My followers, I'm afraid, are relatively humorless types, as you might imagine. So—tell me. What's this ultimate power you offer me?''

Cole paused for a moment, then shouted back, ''An eighty-megaton thermonuclear warhead mounted on an intercontinental ballistic missile, which I can arm and target.''

The man on the ridge said nothing for a moment, then, ''I am called Otis—who knows, we may become great friends.''

Cole's palms stopped sweating and he wiped them, one at a time, along the sides of his fatigue-clad thighs.

Chapter Twenty-Three

Sarah sat in the darkness at the base of an oak tree, Bill Mulliner beside her, the children and Bill's mother further along in the woods with some of Critchfield's men. Pete Critchfield sat opposite her, cross-legged, Indian fashion, shielding one of his foul-smelling cigars with his hand—she knew why. So the glow from the cigar's tip wouldn't show light. She wondered if it had ever occured to Critchfield that an enemy could track him simply by the smell.

"We can't wait none for the Resistance leadership—with David dead or captured—"

"God bless him," Sarah whispered.

"Amen to that," Bill Mulliner intoned.

"Yeah—Amen, but with him out of the picture now, we gotta act. There's a big supply base the Commies are runnin' out of Nashville—been hoardin' stuff there for the last few days. Even more stuff than they had—"

"For what?" Bill asked him.

"Beats the hell outa me, Bill—but they got stuff we need. Medical supplies for openers—I got three men with bad gunshot wounds back in the woods there—no ampicillin or nothin', and no painkiller.

The one guy's so bad, got two fellas sittin' with him to keep his mouth shut if he starts screamin'—been pourin' whiskey into him—"

"It's not a stomach wound, is it?"

"No, ma'am—legs."

"You should be careful—alcohol's a depressant—depressants act funny with blood loss," she told him.

"Well, Sarah—I guess I jes' started a-callin' ya that, ma'am—"

"That's fine—Sarah's my name."

"Well, Sarah—seems to me we could use you helpin' out in two ways—lessen' you got yourself somewheres to go—"

She laughed. "Well, I had a dinner engagement—"

"I'd offer y'all some food, Sarah—but we ain't—"

"I ate this morning," she told him.

"They got food there too at that supply base. If'n you could keep an eye on the wounded, tend to 'em maybe—well, you're pretty good with a gun, too, ma'am. I seen ya, Sarah. You could do that, maybe get your kids to help a might—that'd free up Bill and me and the men to hit that supply depot. We got two trucks stashed out in the woods. We can get to Nashville and be back soon enough—"

"If you come back," she said candidly.

"Well—ain't no arguin' that with ya, Sarah—that's a true fact."

"I'll play nurse," she nodded.

Sometimes, on the other hand, she reflected, being a woman, despite the lack of ego problems, was not such a good thing. "I'll play nurse," she said again.

116

Chapter Twenty-Four

He sat on the ground opposite Otis—the ground was the only place to sit and Otis seemed well at home sitting there, Cole thought.

"You must have a great number of questions."

"Who the hell are you people?" Cole began.

"We are the people who control the entire Pacific Northwest. Anyone who is obviously a stranger here is killed. Those who live here when they are encountered are taken prisoner, given the choice of joining, or dying. Most join. Some die."

"I don't know how many guys you got, Otis—but no way you'd be able to take on a real army."

"That could be a problem someday, I suppose."

Cole watched Otis's eyes in the firelight. They were a light brown color, lighter in shading than Cole had ever imagined a human being's eyes could be. "Someday, you and I maybe'll be enemies, Otis—but now we can be allies. There are six missiles."

"So you have said."

"I need five only—you can have the sixth."

"But Captain Cole—why don't I just kill you and take the missiles?"

"A bomb blast with any conventional explosive you name won't get through those doors into the bunker. Use something too big and you'll destroy the launching equipment inside. And you don't know how to arm the missiles or how to target them. I do, only I do."

"I can have you taken prisoner and tortured, then," Otis smiled. "You see, before the war—I assume it was a war, wasn't it?"

"The United States and Russia—yeah. It was a war."

"Well—before the war, I was arrested and tried for a multiple homicide. I was acquitted—lack of evidence. But I became a cult figure. I was guilty, of course. There were people who wanted to follow me. We came up here, into the mountains, and I was able to live like a tribal chieftain. You see, I studied social anthropology and group dynamics and comparative religions—all that. I made my own religion. This was before the trial. During the trial, the publicity generated caused my star to rise, so to speak. After this—this war, well—it was natural for me to provide order where there was chaos—"

"A religion?"

"More or less—all that is foreign is corrupt, evil. Other races are to be despised—from the cross you burn, I can see you may have heard of such an ideology—"

"The truth is universal," Cole told him.

"Truth? Hardly. But," Otis smiled, "if my followers believe it, I suppose there's no reason you shouldn't too. You see, I ran what the police might call a religious scam—a cult that took money from

118

people for things like prayer shawls, incense, promised miracle cures—we collected many thousands of dollars in money left to us by the faithful. A black gentleman—quite rich—came to me, partook of our prayers and curses—he left his entire fortune to us. A sizable fortune. I broke into his home with two of my—my followers—and I killed him. His whole family, as well, so no one could contest his will. Unfortunately, a neighbor heard the screaming and police arrested us. My two followers committed suicide as I'd ordered them to. The papers were full of racial remarks attributed to me, ideals of racial superiority and a master race—all that drivel. After the acquittal, well—certain types of people were drawn to me. Then this war thing and—well—here we are, aren't we. I mean, I can certainly have you tortured.''

"To tell you stuff, yeah," Cole nodded. "But not to make me actually arm and target the missiles. You could never know if I did it right, could you?"

"I suppose not," Otis laughed. "A man after my own heart. And what do you propose to do with your five missiles?" Otis laughed again. "I mean, if that isn't prying, of course?"

"The Russians occupy much of the East Coast and Midwest—what they didn't bomb out of existence."

"Really—hmmph."

"They use Chicago as their headquarters—"

"A lovely city, Chicago."

"Five eighty-ton warheads will obliterate the entire Soviet High Command in the United States, and tons of supplies, thousands of troops—the land war

119

they're fighting with China is already draining them—they'd never be able to reinvade America and they wouldn't waste their missiles on us—they used most of them during the Night of The War—"

"Is that what you call it?" Otis asked. "Very nice ring to it—the Night of The War. Yes—I like that—I'll incorporate that in my ritual, if you don't object."

"We'd be free again, Otis—kill the fuckin' Commies, then track down the Jews and the niggers that helped 'em along, got them the footholds they needed—make this a country for Americans again."

"Wouldn't many of your Americans—I mean the white, Christian ones—wouldn't they die during this missile strike you propose?"

"Not more than a couple hundred thousand—a million or so at the most—and they'd willingly give their lives if I told them, explained it to them—they would."

"Would they? I wonder."

"They would," Cole told him, trying to reason with him. "First the Commies, then the scum that helped them come to power—get the United States back, build up a supply of warheads again while the Commies fight each other in China—then launch on China and Russia—kill 'em all. Make the world a decent place to live in again. Give our children a world where they can grow up safe—where white girls don't have to—"

"I don't doubt the sincerity of your convictions, captain—but isn't four hundred megatons a bit much for one city?"

"No—we've gotta be sure."

"Yes—we would be sure that way."

"You talked about torture—that man there, the air force colonel—he knows where the bunker is located. If you could—"

"I know where the bunker is located—I always wondered what they kept there. But as to the torture part, well—why don't we give him to my people—they've been so patient. We can let them amuse themselves with him while we discuss some of the fine points of our agreement."

"Then you'll help me to fight for America?"

Cole didn't like Otis—he couldn't understand why the man simply sat there, saying nothing.

Chapter Twenty-Five

Rourke watched the bonfires below him and far to port. It would be the wildmen—perhaps they had trapped Cole, he thought. He heard the voice coming through his headset.

"John—do you see those fires?"

"The wildmen."

"Should we go in?"

Rourke didn't answer her for a moment. Teal could be down there. But if Cole were still in control of his small party of men—and of Teal—Teal would be alive until the missile silos and the control bunker were reached, penetrated. If a stray shot from the wildmen disabled one of these two last functional helicopters, bringing back a full, heavily armed landing party from the submarine would be impossible.

"No, Natalia—we keep going to the coast," he said finally into the small microphone just in front of his lips, a cigar clenched—unlit—in the left corner of his mouth.

"All right," he heard her voice come back. "You are a strange man," her voice sounded in his ear after a moment.

"Why is that?"

"I would have expected you to storm in there—like that story Paul tells about you riding your Harley into the Brigand camp in the desert and killing the leader, then—"

Rourke thought back—it seemed so long ago. He remembered Paul then—like two different people in terms of skills and abilities. He studied the lights on the instrument panels. "That served a purpose," he told her.

"Revenge?"

"Yes."

"And now the purpose is—" She let the question hang.

"Keep Cole from launching those missiles—it's the only thing he can be planning. The only thing. Millions of lives maybe—against one life."

He wondered if Armand Teal would understand. Rourke smiled to himself—he wondered if he himself understood it.

Chapter Twenty-Six

It felt primitive—that was the word, Cole thought. "Primitive," and he verbalized it, watching Teal, tied to one of the crosses, a large man using a knife whose blade gleamed orange in the firelight near the foot of the cross, slicing skin in narrow strips from Armand Teal's legs.

Teal had stopped screaming, only moaning incoherently now as the knife edged slowly upward.

"It's an art—like everything done with skill," Otis explained, standing beside him. "To torture without inducing total unconsciousness or death is a precision craft. My man Forrester does it with such consummate grace—I rarely tire of watching him. He seems always to find a new and more subtle variation—oh, there—watch!"

Otis was gesturing now, enthused for the first time since Cole had seen him.

Cole watched, too.

Forrester was holding the naked Teal's testicles, using a different knife now—small-seeming. "That's as sharp as a razor—as they say," Otis whispered conspiratorially and smiled. "What he's doing I've only seen him do once before—it's wonderful."

Cole thought Otis was insane—but he watched anyway, almost compelled to. The man with the knife—the one Otis had called Forrester—was seemingly shaving Teal's testicles.

"He's removing the upper layer of skin—but so slowly and patiently as to prevent most bleeding. Then—after that, he'll move to the—"

"I don't wanna—"

"Ohh—but it's exquisite. One of the women will come up to him—arouse him—and—well, he bleeds to death, captain—"

Cole turned his face away—he threw up across the top of his combat boots.

"Really, captain—for a man who wishes to slaughter so many—well, I hardly see where this should be—"

Cole turned and looked at Otis, the gleam in his light brown eyes. He did not look at Armand Teal.

He closed his eyes, hearing a woman's voice, hearing Teal moaning—then hearing a scream after a very long time.

There was something half a chant, half a cheer coming from the self-imposed darkness around him.

Otis' voice sounded in a whisper at his ear. He could feel the man's breath—it smelled like marijuana. "It's over now, captain—you can open your eyes."

Cole opened his eyes. Otis had lied. It wasn't over. And he heard Otis laugh.

Chapter Twenty-Seven

Rourke hung back, his complement of the shore party boarded on his chopper, Natalia—her craft landed on the missile deck of the submarine—still loading. Gundersen spoke to him through his headset. "You get these men back, Rourke—otherwise I won't have enough manpower to run my little boat."

Rourke laughed into the microphone. "Little boat?"

"Well—you got me straight, though?"

"I understand," Rourke said into his microphone. The sea was rough, a wind blowing in off the mainland now, a wind that would make headwinds he'd have to fight in returning to Paul and Lieutenant O'Neal. The sea itself was gray, whitecaps dotting it like freckles on a child's face. "You got any idea what the weather is looking like, commander?"

"Negative on that—at least beyond the fact that it looks crappy from here."

"You sound just like a professional meteorologist."

"It's worse for me—I open up a window, I get

127

my feet wet—submarines are like that."

Rourke shook his head, saying, "Standup comic before you joined the navy?"

"No—but thanks for the compliment."

"I wasn't making a compliment," Rourke told him. Because of cross winds, it had been rough landing on the missile deck—rougher by the time Natalia had done it. And now—the winds visibly rising as the waves tossed higher and higher—it would be hazardous in the extreme to take off. This was why he waited—if the helicopter ran into problems he would be there to fish out survivors.

"Natalia—you reading me?"

"Yes, John. Over."

"Don't be so formal—only you and me and Gundersen on the line here. How you reading those winds?"

"Twenty-five knots and gusting higher."

"Rourke?" It was Gundersen. "I'm gonna have to dive soon—these seas are getting rough. I've got some people in sick bay this is playin' hell with."

"Got ya," Rourke answered. "Natalia? How long?"

"Another minute—maybe two. The deck is slippery—we're using guidelines to get the men out to the helicopter."

"Right," he told her, watching her craft now—tense. From his vantage point two hundred feet up and to the sub's starboard side, Rourke could see what seemed to be the last two men, struggling along the missile deck on the manilla rope guidelines, wind lashing at the raingear the men wore against the salt spray that broke over the bow as the submarine lurched violently with each swell.

The last of the two men disappeared inside the helicopter Natalia piloted. She was a good aviatrix, Rourke knew—but the best helicopter pilot in the world would have been hard-pressed to judge his controls right to get off the swaying, rolling missile deck against the wind.

The helicopter—as if a living thing itself—began to move, rising slightly, edging forward and to the right side, then rising more, spinning several times then dipping slightly downward—Rourke's heart went to his mouth—then skimmed along the surface of the waves, then was airborne.

"She flies good." Gundersen's voice echoed through his headset.

Rourke chewed down harder on his unlit cigar. "Yeah," he murmured.

Chapter Twenty-Eight

Paul Rubenstein sat cross-legged in the rocks, his head bothering him slightly. "The hell with it," he murmured, reaching into the pocket of his O.D. green field jacket, finding the container Rourke had given him and removing one of the painkillers Rourke had prescribed. The octagon-sided tablet in his mouth, he splashed it down with a swallow of canteen water. "Lieutenant?"

"Yes, Mr. Rubenstein?" And O'Neal turned toward him. O'Neal's M-16 was nearly to the level of the rocks, ready to come up to fire.

"When John gave me these for pain, he told me to try and rest for a few minutes after I took one—do me a favor and keep a good eye out—I gotta close my eyes—my head's killing me."

"Right, Mr. Rubenstein."

Rubenstein nodded, then hunkered down in the rocks. The bolt was closed on the Schmeisser and his High Power was holstered. Rourke had often lectured on mixing firearms with any type of depressant or stimulant—with any foreign substance—and Rubenstein took the advice seriously. Having had, for all intents and purposes, no familiarity with firearms before the Night of The War, he now considered himself well-skilled—he'd had what he considered the best teacher. But firearms were not second nature to him as they were to Rourke. Almost subconsciously, he took advice literally and intended to until more familiarity deepened his judgment.

He set the Schmeisser aside on the ground next to him, folding his hands in his lap. He stretched his legs, tired from the sleepless night. He saw a face—she had been his girl. He wondered if all the people who inhabited New York City had died quickly. . . .

"Mr. Rubenstein! Mr. Rubenstein—Paul!"

She had been so pretty in a very soft way—he didn't want to lose—

"Mr. Rubenstein! Wake up!"

Rubenstein opened his eyes, feeling warm, sleepy still, then moved, suddenly feeling the cold and dampness, his eyes reacting to the bright grayness of the morning.

"How—ahh—how long—"

"About three-quarters of an hour maybe—look, Mr. Rubenstein."

Paul shook his head, snatching up his Schmeisser, then getting to his knees—the headache was gone—and peering over the rocks.

Across the small depression where the mounded-over bunker was on the far ridge he could see wildmen massing. And now, faintly, he could hear the rumbling of vehicles.

He could see the first one—a battered Jeep—rolling up onto his far left on the ridge. Then, on his right, another Jeep.

And then at the center—a massive pickup truck, the wheels high off the ground and suspended from the winch supports at the front of the vehicle was a body—burned black in spots, blood covered, the left arm missing, the eyes catching the glint of sunlight and reflecting it like glass—it was Armand Teal.

"Look!"

"I see him," Rubenstein murmured to O'Neal.

"No—no—look!"

Rubenstein turned his head right, toward O'Neal, then past him. Wildmen behind them, wildmen on either side, heavily armed with assault rifles, spears and machetes, some of the wildmen standing like toy figurines, almost frozen, their spears poised for flight.

And at their head—"Cole—you son of a bitch!"

"Mr. Rubenstein—you and Lieutenant O'Neal—lay down your arms," Cole shouted.

"Bullshit!"

"Lay down your arms and you'll be spared—at least for now. I came for the missiles—not to kill you!"

Rubenstein worked back the bolt of the Schmeisser, pushing O'Neal aside, on his knees still, the submachine gun snaking forward. He saw it—the shadowy form in flight as he fired, Cole dodging, two of the wildmen with him going down.

Something—the shadowy thing that flew—was in his line of vision, tearing into him now, dragging him back and off his knees. He felt himself spread-eagling, his subgun still firing, upward, his left arm

133

unmoving. He stared at his arm—a massive stick seemed to be holding him to the ground.

"The spear—my God, Mr. Rubenstein!"

It was O'Neal.

"Spear—" Rubenstein coughed the word, his subgun firing out. He tried to move his left arm, felt the tearing, the ripping at his flesh. "No!" He screamed the word.

Chapter Twenty-Nine

Bill Mulliner squirmed on his knees beside the right front wheel of the van—it was his stomach. His father—the Russians had killed him—had called it "butterflies," and Bill Mulliner had them every time before a raid. As soon as the raid would start, the butterflies left. He wondered if it was fear of death—or fear of what came afterward. In church on Sundays they used to talk about the glory that awaited you when you had been born again in Jesus Christ, the glory of Heaven when you never wanted, never needed, but were filled with the happiness of being in God's presence. He wondered sometimes how you could be happy with the life gone from you. Or was the life something that wasn't physical at all?

He gripped his M-16 more tightly.

He looked to his left and up. Just inside the slid-open door of the van he could see the heels of Pete Critchfield's shoes—Pete would be hunkered down low, waiting, his M-16 with the collapsible butt stock—admittedly homemade—ready to kill Russians.

Bill Mulliner looked to his far right and down. In

135

the drainage ditch on the other side of the fence, already penetrated past Russian security, would be Curly and Jim, Jim with a Thompson submachine gun. He'd been a police officer before the Night of The War and the weapon had been legal and licensed.

The others—fifteen additional men, making nineteen all told, were scattered along the base perimeter. All of them were waiting for the signal.

The base had been, according to Pete Critchfield, a recording company warehouse. The security system in use when the facility had stored the latest country western albums was the security system in use today. Only the manpower composition and numbers had changed. Two older, retired policemen had been the security guards on the day shift—this according to Jim Hastings, the cop with the Thompson. Now, however, there were thirty-six Russian infantrymen with KGB supervision who patrolled the facility's fenced perimeter with guard dogs.

It would be Jim who would give the signal—waiting until a truck marked as carrying explosives would enter the compound. Jim would throw a fragmentation grenade—between the nineteen men, there were only four grenades. The battle would start.

Bill Mulliner watched now, a motorcycle escort rolling along the street ahead of a U.S. two-and-one-half-ton truck, the truck overpainted with a red star on the door side, he could see. The motorcyclists were talking to each other, one of them gesturing to an abandoned Mercedes parked half across the sidewalk. The second cyclist laughed. A joke about capitalist Americans, Bill guessed.

His palms sweated, as much as they had sweated when Jim Hastings and Curly had smuggled themselves into the compound inside a garbage truck, then jumped from the truck—he had seen one of them barely at the far corner of the warehouse.

The deuce-and-half made a sharp, fast right—Bill Mulliner thought he would never drive that way carrying explosives—and turned into the driveway leading into the warehouse area, stopping in front of the fence, the guards there approaching the fence and opening it. The motorcyclists started through, the truck's transmission grinding audibly, black smoke belching from the muffler, the truck beginning to lumber forward.

Automatically, Bill Mulliner moved his selector from safe to full auto, then glanced to his right. He could see Jim Hastings starting to get up in the ditch, his right arm hauling back, then snapping half-forward. There was a small dark object—Bill watched it fascinated as it arced toward the truck through the late morning air.

The grenade fell—he could hear the noise it made hitting the concrete. It rolled, and he watched it, waiting for it to explode. Waiting.

The explosions were something that made his ears ring and his head ache, the first tiny explosion of the grenade swallowed by the roar and blast of the truck itself, a black and orange fireball belching skyward. He started to run from behind the van, the heat of the fireball searingly hot against his face as a wind seemed to generate from the fireball above and

137

surrounding the explosives truck.

He was at the main gates—what was left of them, jumping from a fallen motorcycle, loosing a three-round burst from his M-16 into the already half-dead cycle rider, the man's clothes and flesh burning as he rolled, screaming, on the ground. The tarred surface under Bill's feet stuck to his shoes, the tar melting from the heat of the fireball as he ran. He glanced behind him once—he could see Pete Critchfield coming with the van, the van's front end specially reinforced, the van jumping the curb, across the sidewalk now and ramming through the chain link fence, a seven-foot-wide section of the fencing pulling away from the support posts—these bent almost in half—and stuck to the reinforced bumper, pushing ahead of the van, sparks flying from the fencing as it swept the concrete.

Bill kept running, seeing a sentry coming toward him, the sentry's guard dog bounding ahead. Bill pumped the M-16's trigger, the dog still coming. He pumped the trigger again, the dog going down. The sentry still firing, his AK-47 hammering slugs into the warehouse wall beside which Bill ran, the concrete block powdering, chips of the concrete and a spray of fine dust powdering Bill's face.

Bill fired the M-16, hearing the heavier rattle of the Thompson submachine gun, seeing Jim Hastings running to intersect him. The Soviet guard went down.

Bill ran forward, jumping the dead guard, firing his M-16, two guards coming around the far corner of the warehouse wall, one guard going down, a long burst of automatic weapons fire hammering into the wall again, the second guard tucking back.

Bill heard the scraping of the chain link fence section, the roar of the van's eight-cylinder engine, saw the blur of grayish white as the van cut past him and toward the corner of the building. There was a scream, the sound of tires screeching and a power steering unit being pushed too hard, then the blur of gray-white again, the van backing up. The fence was still stuck to the bumper, and hanging from it now was a body—the Soviet trooper, his hands flailing, his legs twisted at odd angles.

Jim Hastings—less than a yard from Bill now, raised his Thompson to his shoulder, firing a short burst, the Soviet guard's body stopping its thrashing—he was dead.

There was assault rifle fire all around him now as he reached the corner of the warehouse, the van already by the loading dock, some of the Resistance fighters there too, M-16s, pistols, riot shotguns—gunfire.

Bill threw himself against the loading dock, ramming a fresh magazine into his assault rifle, then looked up, across the loading dock, throwing his body up, rolling, coming to his knees and firing as two Soviet soldiers started across. Both Soviets went down.

He pushed himself to his feet, Jim Hastings and Curly already opening the sliding door into the warehouse itself.

Hastings and Curly disappeared inside, Bill running to the truck, Pete Critchfield jumping out, his bastardized M-16 in his fists.

"So far so good, Bill."

Bill Mulliner looked at his leader. "Yeah—so far so good."

The butterflies were gone from his stomach and he was still alive—so far, so good.

Chapter Thirty

The airfield in the shadow of Mount Thunder was busy—as busy, he supposed, as airfields had appeared during the Berlin airlift the Allies had conducted when his own government had shut off West Berlin from West Germany years ago. Planes of any description that could carry cargo were landing, being off-loaded and refueled simultaneously and taking off again as quickly as possible.

Rozhdestvenskiy walked the field now, an aide running to his side, the aide falling in step, shouting to him over the roar of the engines. "Comrade Colonel—a communique from the southeast."

"Read it to me," Rozhdestvenskiy nodded. Probably another complaint that some item of supply could not be found, he thought.

"Central southeastern supply depot, reference Womb, penetrated by heavily armed, numerically superior Resistance force. Heavy casualties and theft of strategic material and supplies—preliminary casualty report and loss report to follow—signed—"

"Never mind—I know the fool's name!" He took the note, crumpled it, started to throw it down to the runway surface—he stopped himself. His temper—he was losing it, and thus showing a weakness before a subordinate. "He is a fool," he sighed, by way of explanation, "in that he allows himself such a situation to come to pass—to—"

"Yes, Comrade Colonel!"

He studied the subordinate's face. There was little apparent differences in their ages—yet this man was a captain and he was a colonel. The face, however, showed the difference. Moon-shaped, fleshy, ingratiating—weak.

He was not weak.

"You will radio immediately to the commander of the supply depot in Nashville—he is to place himself under arrest and surrender command to his senior ranking subordinate. You will radio Chicago that I am to be met at the airport and there must be a helicopter to fly me to headquarters on the Lake. You will also radio to General Varakov, supreme commander, that it is a matter of the utmost urgency that I should have an interview with him immediately. Make all necessary travel arrangements, contact my valet here and have my things packed for a short stay. Move out."

"Yes, Comrade Colonel."

The man ran off, across the field—like a dog more than a man, Rozhdestvenskiy decided. There was the difference.

He would go to Chicago, request that General Varakov commit his military forces to crush the Resistance so the stocking of the Womb could continue. He would request Varakov's help in resolving the matter of the American Eden Project—

He felt himself smile. If Varakov did not cooper-

142

ate—

Colonel Nehemiah Rozhdestvenskiy watched the planes as they landed, as they took off again—for at least a few moments.

The efficient, orderly use of power.

It would calm him.

Chapter Thirty-One

Rourke calculated his fuel use to be adequate to make the return trip to the submarine—beyond that perhaps enough to make it back to where he had camouflaged the prototype FB-111HX for the return trip to Georgia—if his luck held. He flew the OH58C Kiowas now at maximum speed, not the speed for fuel conservation, but the speed required by the situation. He had been gone from the missile control bunker and the underground silos vastly longer than he had anticipated. He glanced to his right—the dull green of the second helicopter was there, Natalia almost visible at its controls.

They flew low to give as little advance warning of their arrival as possible, in case somehow, something had gone wrong. He followed the contours of the ground with his altimeter, rising over a low ridge.

In the distance he could see that something had gone wrong.

Wildmen were everywhere, and at their center were two crosses—O'Neal and Rubenstein?

He overflew the crosses, glancing below him now—Paul, perhaps dead, certainly close to unconsciousness. O'Neal, his body twisting against the ropes that bound him to the cross timbers.

Near the crosses, he could see Cole, Cole's two men Armitage and Kelsoe, and a bizarre, squat-looking man wrapped in a bearskin robe. Cole beckoned to the sky—Rourke knew why.

"Natalia—"

"Yes—I see—do we go in?"

"We pull back along the other side of that ridge line," he said into his microphone. "Then I go in—that's what Cole wants." He exhaled hard into the microphone. "And that's what Cole is going to get."

Rourke banked the chopper sharply, shouting past his microphone to the men near the open chopper doors, "Hang on to the seats, guys—" He chewed harder on his cigar. . . .

The rotor blades from Natalia's helicopter still moved lazily in the breeze, but it was not the breeze that moved them. Natalia stood beside him, dressed in her dark clothing and boots, her pistols on her hips, seeming to accentuate their roundness—she had trained to be a ballerina, she had told him once, and her martial arts skills were past the level of the ordinary and almost elevated to the artistry of the dance. There was a perfection about her—he saw her eyes quickly flicker to his—their blueness overwhelming him. He turned away, looking at the men of the shore party.

"A lot of you saw Lieutenant O'Neal strung up on that cross down there. The other man most of you know—he's my best friend, Paul Rubenstein. So we've all got a very personal stake in getting

146

them out alive if we can. I didn't see Colonel Teal. If Cole and the wildmen have formed some kind of alliance, then Teal might already be dead. I don't know who this Cole is—but I know what he is. In his own way, he's more of a savage than those wildmen we've been fighting, you've been hearing about. I recognize some of you from the landing party that night that came in with Gundersen. So you know how these people are—crazy, suicidal—deadly.

"I have to go in—Cole wants it that way, and if we all go in shooting, Paul and your lieutenant will be killed—they'd do that. Cole would. I know it. Natalia is staying here—"

"No," she snapped, almost hissing the word. Their eyes met.

"Yes," he ordered. "Major Tiemerovna is a pilot—we need at least one here to cover you guys from the air. You'll have to break up into two elements—one Natalia can fly in over the wildmen, drop on the far side. That way you'll have them set up for a kind of enclosement—if you do it right. Natalia'll need a gunner—"

"I'm the man who runs the deck gun on the submarine."

"Then you're the man," Rourke told the young, blond-haired seaman with the oddly brushed mustache. Rourke supposed the young man had grown it either to show he could or to look older. "Then Natalia and you'll give air support. We'll need one man to stay with the second helicopter—the one I flew. If the wildmen break through, put a burst into the machine—Natalia'll show you where to shoot so

147

you can blow her up. In case Cole or one of his men knows how to use a chopper, we can't let him have it. If you do blow the chopper, run like hell and you're on your own. Volunteer?''

Three men took a step forward. Rourke picked one—a seaman first he'd seen in the fighting on the beach against the wildmen—he seemed to have a cool head. ''You're it, Schmulowitz.''

''Aye, sir.''

''Natalia'll pick squad leaders for the ground action—do exactly as she says. If any ten of you guys had between you as much battle experience as she has, you'd be doin' great.''

''And what about you?'' Natalia asked him suddenly.

Rourke swung the CAR-15 forward on its cross-bodied sling, the scope covers removed already, the stock extended.

He unzipped the front of his bomber jacket so he could get at his pistols. He reached into his pocket and took out the little Freedom Arms .22 Magnum Boot pistol with the three-inch barrel, the one he'd taken off the dead Brigand back in Georgia before they had met Cole, before Natalia had been wounded and they had been forced to take to the nuclear submarine, then transported under the icepack to the new west coast—before he had ever heard of wildmen.

He slipped the pistol up his left sleeve, just inside the storm-sleeved cuff.

''I'll go see what Cole wants—try to get something going with Paul and O'Neal—I'll be there.''

He reached into his jeans pocket, found his Zippo

lighter, turned it over in his hands a moment and flicked back the cowling, rolling the striking wheel under his thumb, making the blue-yellow flame appear, the flame flickering in the breeze as he lit the cigar clamped between his teeth.

"I'll be okay," he said. Her eyes didn't look like she believed it.

Chapter Thirty-Two

Rourke walked slowly ahead, having stopped for a moment at the top of the rise, looked down toward the missile bunker—a half-dozen wildmen were posted there as sentries—and then stared at the crosses. Rubenstein was still unmoving, his left arm red-stained along the entire length of the sleeve of his jacket. O'Neal had stopped moving, and Rourke saw the man's eyes at the distance—pain and fear.

He kept walking.

He reached the height of the rise, beside the twin crude crosses, and stopped. He reached out with his right hand, feeling Paul's ankles for a pulse—there was one.

"Give me your guns." A wildman, large, armed with an AK-47—where he'd gotten it Rourke didn't know—stepped from the far side of the crosses and reached out his left hand.

Rourke, the cigar in the left corner of his mouth, reached up his left hand and took the cigar. He stared at the wildman's hand for a moment, cleared his throat and spit, the glob of spittle hitting the wildman's palm.

"You son of a bitch," the man snarled, Rourke

sidestepping half-left and wheeling, his left foot snapping up, feigning a kick at the head, the wildman dodging to his left, Rourke's right, leaning forward, Rourke wheeling right, both fists knotted on the CAR-15, his right fist pumping forward with the butt of the rifle, the rifle butt snapping into the wildman's chest, Rourke arcing the flash-deflectored muzzle down diagonally left to right across the man's nose, breaking it at the bridge.

Rourke stepped back, short of killing him, his right foot stomping on the barrel of the AK-47 as the wildman—huge-seeming even in collapse—tumbled forward and sprawled across the ground.

The wildmen were starting to move, Rourke's rifle's muzzle on line with Cole. "Call em off, asshole!"

"They'll rip you apart," Cole shouted back.

"Let's see what the man wants first, shall we?"

Rourke shifted his eyes left—to the man in the bearskin, the squat man he had seen beside Cole from the air. "Cut 'em both down—now!"

"No!"

Rourke's eyes met Cole's eyes. "You're a dead man already—on borrowed time."

"Cut them down," the squat man in the bearskin commanded.

Rourke stepped back, his eyes flickering from Cole to the wildmen starting toward the two crosses.

A burly, tall man started up the cross where Rubenstein hung, hacking at the ropes, Rourke snarling to him, "Let him down easy or you get a gut full of this," and he gestured with the CAR-15.

The man climbing the cross looked at him, nodding almost imperceptibly.

Others of the wildmen started forward, catching Rubenstein as the ropes were released, helping him down, setting him on the ground. Rourke shot a glance to his friend's face. The eyelids fluttered, opened, the lips—parched-seeming—parted and—the voice weak—Rubenstein murmured, "John?"

"Yeah, Paul," Rourke almost whispered. "It's okay."

"I'm-I'm gettin'—"

"Take it easy," Rourke told him, watching Cole and shifting his eyes to O'Neal as they brought him down from the cross.

"I'm dyin' on my feet, damnit!"

Rourke looked at his friend, edging toward him, gesturing the wildmen away with the muzzle of the CAR-15, then snapping, "Get ready," reaching down, helping Rubenstein's right arm across his shoulders, getting the younger man up, slumping against his left side. "All right?"

"Yeah," Rubenstein sighed. "Yeah—all right."

Rourke said nothing, looking at O'Neal, lying there—O'Neal seemed somehow more subdued, more ill than when he had been on the cross—his eyelids closed and his head slumped. Rourke caught the movement of a pulse—strong-seeming—in the missile officer's neck.

O'Neal was playing out something—Rourke let the young navy lieutenant play it out."

"Okay, Paul—we start forward—right?"

"Right," Rubenstein nodded, his breath coming in short gasps, but regular.

153

Rourke started to walk, half dragging his friend on his left side, the CAR-15's muzzle leveled now toward Cole and the squat man in the bearskin and Levis.

He kept the muzzle in the airspace between them, already decided that if either one moved, he'd shoot the man in the bearskin first.

The wildmen—a knot of them—closed around Rourke and Rubenstein as they moved forward.

"You'll never get outa here alive, you Jew-lovin'—"

"Shove it, Cole," Rourke snarled.

Then Rourke stopped, less than two yards of airspace separating him and Paul from Cole and the man in the bearskin.

"I'm called Otis," the man in the bearskin smiled.

"No shit," Rourke nodded.

"You are—ah?"

"He's John Rourke—Dr. Rourke," Cole said through his teeth.

"Ohh—the John Rourke who wrote those excellent texts on wilderness survival—how marvelous. To meet you after reading your work—I literally devoured them. And the books on weapons as well—"

"Marvelous," Rourke told him.

"Since I know so much about you—I suppose—well, that you'd like to know something about me—and about my little band of followers here."

Rourke said nothing.

"He's looney, John," Rubenstein coughed.

Rourke still said nothing.

"We actually call ourselves the Brotherhood of

154

The Pure Fire. I'm the high priest, the spiritual leader—the mentor to these lost souls, one might say."

"One might," Rourke whispered.

"Yes—well, as you can imagine, after all this war business, well—the time was ripe for someone—"

"To appoint himself leader of the crazies," Rourke interrupted.

Otis—the wildman leader—smiled. "In a manner of speaking—I suppose so. But of course our mutual friend here—I think he makes me seem mild. After all—blowing up Chicago with five eighty-megaton warheads is a bit extreme, isn't it?"

Rourke's eyes shifted to Cole's eyes—Cole's eyes like pinpoints of black light burning into him.

"Now's the time you're supposed to say, 'You'll never get away with this,' " and Cole laughed. "But I'm more of a patriot than you—hangin' around with Jews and Commies. I'm gonna rid the United States of the Soviet High Command."

"President Chambers never sent you, did he—neither did Reed."

"Reed? Hell—I almost hadda shoot Reed when I killed the real Cole and took his orders—bullshit with Reed. Him and Chambers—they'd never have the nerve to push a button—but me—"

Rourke said nothing. He looked at Paul once, murmuring, "Good-bye old friend," then pumped the trigger of the CAR-15, in and out and in and out and in and out, three fast rounds in a burst to Cole's chest, Cole—or whoever he really was—falling back, screaming, his hands flaying out at his sides.

"My missile!" Otis screamed, his voice like a high-pitched feminine shriek, a broad-bladed knife flashing into his right hand from a sheath at his belt. Rourke shifted the muzzle of the CAR-15 left, firing, but Otis was diving toward him, the slug impacting against Otis' right shoulder, hammering the man back and down, but not killing him, Rourke realized.

As Otis fell back, his body rolled against a mounded tarp behind him, part of the tarp whisking back—Teal's burned and mutilated body, the eyes still open in death—was on the ground, insects crawling across the face.

The wildmen were closing in, knives, spears, assault rifles in every hand. There was gunfire—from the edge of the rise near the crosses.

Rourke pumped the CAR-15's trigger, unable to miss, firing into a solid wall of humanity, Rubenstein lurching away from him, Rourke feeling the rip and hearing the snap as the younger man grabbed the Detonics .45 from under Rourke's left armpit, the heavy bark of the .45 rumbling too now, the gunfire from their rear unmistakably that of an AK-47—"O'Neal!" Rourke shouted.

Rourke fired out the CAR-15, ramming the muzzle of the empty gun into a face near him, with his left hand snatching at the Detonics .45 under his right armpit, thumbing back the hammer, firing point blank into the face of the nearest wildman, the body sprawling back, others falling from its weight.

Rourke's right hand flashed to the flap holster on his hip, getting the Python, the six-inch barrel snaking forward, the pistol bucking slightly in his clenched right fist as the muzzle flashed fire, the nearest wildman clasping his neck.

"John—here!"

It was Rubenstein's voice, Rourke edging back, firing both handguns now, the Detonics in his left—loaded with seven rounds this time—and the Colt in his right—loaded with six.

Both guns were half-spent as he edged back from the knot of screaming, howling wildmen. He looked skyward for an instance, the heavy, hollow chopping sound of helicopter rotor blades suddenly loud over the shouts of the men trying to kill him.

"Natalia!" he shouted.

The green OH58C helicopter was coming in low, and now fire was spitting from the side gun, the 7.62mm slugs hammering into the knot of wildmen, their shrieks louder now as they ran for cover.

"Over here, John!"

Rourke looked behind him, Rubenstein beside a massive pickup truck. Rourke started to run toward him, the Python bucking in Rourke's right fist as he snapped the last three shots over his left shoulder, then threw himself into a run, automatic weapons fire already starting around him, then dove for the shelter of the vehicle.

Rubenstein—on his knees, pale as death beside the right front wheel-well, fired the Detonics. "Empty."

Rourke slammed closed the cylinder of the Python, the Safariland speedloader, empty now, crammed back into his musette bag. He handed the pistol to Rubenstein. "Here—use this."

Rourke took the Detonics, emptying his own pistol, then reloading both with fresh magazines from the Sparks six pack on his belt.

He reached into the musette bag, finding a spare magazine for the CAR-15, dumping the empty, ramming the fresh one home, working the bolt, then passing the rifle to Rubenstein, the Python out of ammo. Rourke took another of the Safariland speedloaders, reloaded the big Colt and holstered the gun.

He reached into the musette bag, getting the remaining loaded magazines for the CAR-15, putting them on the ground beside Paul. "You recovered fast—"

"Bullshit—I'm dying—just too stupid to fall down."

"Lemme look at that," and Rourke slipped behind the younger man, probing gently at the wound. Rourke reached behind him, snatching the AG Russell Sting IA from the sheath at his belt, using the blade to cut away the sleeve.

"Aww—that was my good coat, John."

"Shut up," Rourke snapped—the wound was dirty, clotted—he would have to open it to clean it. "You think it hurts now—wait'll I get around to fixin' it!"

Rubenstein glanced at him, then pushed his wire-rimmed glasses back up the bridge of his nose. "Coulda been worse, John—coulda lost my glasses."

"Yeah—could've at that," Rourke told him, leaning against the pickup truck. "Remember how to hotwire a car?"

"Yeah—I remember," Rubenstein nodded.

"Gimme that rifle and climb up there—once you've got it going, I'll pass up the CAR and the spare mags—we take off for the bunker—make a stand there—run over as many people as we can on the way, huh?"

Rubenstein smiled, handed Rourke the rifle and reached up for the door handle.

"Shit—it's locked!"

"I'll fix that," Rourke told him. "Look away." Rourke reached for the Python at his hip, aimed at the lock and turned his face away, firing upward, the thudding sound loud of lead against sheet metal. "Now try it."

Rubenstein pulled at the door handle—"Hot" and the handle broke away, the door swinging out.

The younger man grinned, then started up into the pickup cab, gunfire coming from the sky again as Natalia's helicopter made another pass, gunfire from the ground as well as the shore party advanced from both sides. Rourke looked under the truck now, finding targets of opportunity with the CAR-15, firing single shots into backs and chests and legs, bringing down as many of the wildmen as he could.

The truck vibrated, coughed, rumbled—the engine made sputtering sounds as it came to life.

"John!"

"Right," and Rourke edged up, grabbing the spare magazines, then throwing himself up beside Rubenstein. "Can you drive this thing one-handed?"

"You just shift when I tell ya to," Rubenstein shouted.

"Right," and Rourke, the Python back in his right fist, tugged at the door, closing it partially.

Wildmen running for the truck, Rourke's right hand swinging the Python on line—one round, a head shot. A man down. Another round, then another, two in the chest and a man down. He fired out the last two, a double shot at a wildman with an M-16, the rifle discharging a long, ragged burst, a spiderwebbing in the glass at the top of the windshield.

"Shit," Rubenstein shouted, the truck starting to move.

Rourke holstered the empty Python, giving Rubenstein the CAR-15. "Just aim the truck forward and hold the wheel with your left knee—"

"Gotchya, John," Rubenstein called back, taking the CAR-15 in his right fist and pointing it out the window, firing as wildmen stormed toward them.

Rourke took one of the Detonics pistols, firing point blank as a wildman jumped for the hood of the truck, the face exploding, blood caught on the truck's slipstream spattering the windshield.

The truck lumbered ahead. "Have to shift," Rubenstein shouted.

Rourke's left hand reached to the stick, his concentration focused on hearing, feeling the clutch pedal activate. He upshifted into second, the vehicle starting to weave, then back under control, no firing from Rubenstein with the CAR.

Rourke—through the partially shattered windshield—could see the bunker now—and there was a man near to it, near the doors, the doors opening—

"Cole!"

Chapter Thirty-Three

Natalia glanced at her altimeter and banked the helicopter to port, checking her degrees against the level horizon, correcting slightly and banking again, homing the machine toward the greatest concentration of wildmen, around the massive, oversize-wheeled pickup truck that she could see Rubenstein driving, Rourke beside him. At the far end of the flat expanse along the ridge she could see Lieutenant O'Neal as well—the rifle in his hands a familiar shape—an AK-47.

"Gunner—start firing when you're ready—leveling off," she shouted back.

"Yes, ma'am," the blond seaman shouted.

And she could hear it—the rattling of the M-60 machine gun mounted in the door—for his sake she wished there had been flak gear to protect his legs. There was heavy fire coming again from the ground as he strafed the wildmen attacking the truck.

Her heart froze—a man was entering the missile control bunker—Cole.

She pulled up on the controls, gaining altitude so she could maneuver, banking the helicopter steeply, "Hold on, gunner!"

161

"Yes, ma'am—holdin' on!"

The helicopter spun a full one hundred eighty degrees and she had the nose lined up on the bunker, throttling out toward it, arcing hard to starboard. "Gunner—kill that man entering the bunker!"

There was no answer in words, just the rattle of the M-60 machine gun, Natalia watching as the gun walked on target, the ground plowing up under the impact of the slugs, Cole disappearing inside the bunker doors as bullets hammered against the concrete surrounding the doors and into the doors themselves, Cole gone.

"Damnit!" she snapped. She pulled up on the controls, banking steeply to starboard again, climbing, then nosing down toward the ground—she would have to get the wildmen on the ground blocking Rourke and Rubenstein in the truck—and Rourke and Paul would have to get Cole. "Damnit!"

Chapter Thirty-Four

Rourke rammed a fresh magazine into each of the Detonics pistols, shoving both out the window simultaneously as a wildman carrying a machete threw himself across the hood of the truck, Rubenstein screaming, "John!"

Rourke fired both pistols, the slugs impacting against the blond, burly wildman's curly-haired chest, the body rolling off the front of the hood, Rourke bouncing in his seat, his head hitting the roof of the truck cab as the vehicle rolled over the body and there was a hideous-sounding scream.

The bunker was less than a hundred yards away now, Rourke firing at targets of opportunity, occasionally the truck lurching under him as Rubenstein would free his right hand to pump the CAR-15 through the driver's side window.

And Cole had disappeared.

Natalia's chopper buzzed overhead, gunfire pouring from it into the surrounding wildmen attempting to stop the truck through sheer force of body numbers, a solid wall forming in front of Rourke and Rubenstein, gunfire everywhere now, from the wildmen and from the submarine's shore

163

party.

At the doors of the bunker now Rourke could see a second figure—O'Neal. The missile officer was stepping back, kicking out, ramming his foot against the outer door of the bunker, then falling onto his knees, firing his pirated AK-47 at the locking mechanism.

Rourke pumped the triggers of the twin stainless Detonics pistols, the truck grinding ahead, over the bodies, hurtling bodies to each side, gunfire ripping into the windshield again. Rourke fired out both pistols, nailing the wildman with the assault rifle.

Forty yards to go, Rourke ramming fresh magazines into his pistols. He fired one pistol through the open side window, killing a man there, then pushed open the door, standing up, holding to the truck cab, shouting to O'Neal, "Back away—we're gonna ram the door." The massive winch at the front of the vehicle—it could be used as a battering ram, Rourke judged. "Paul—get into a crouch behind the wheel—I'll jump clear. Leave her in second and give her all the gas you got!"

"Right—gotchya," Rubenstein shouted back.

Rourke jammed the second Detonics into his left hip pocket, holding on now against the window frame with his left fist, leaning out, firing the Detonics pistol in his right, a chest shot on a woman with a spear rushing toward them, her blond hair knotted and tangled, dirty. Her body spun out and she fell, lurching forward, the truck bouncing as the right front wheel crushed her, a scream piercing the air.

Rourke fired again—twenty-five yards to go—a

massive man wrapped in what looked like dog skins racing toward them firing an assault rifle. Rourke emptied the Detonics into the man's chest and neck, bright splotches of blood flowing there, the body lurching back, falling against more of the wildmen in his wake.

The Detonics was empty, the slide locked open, a wildman rushing them with a machete. Rourke dodged the machete as the man hurtled himself laterally across the hood, Rourke's right fist arcing out with the Detonics still clenched there, using the butt of the pistol like a piece of pipe or a roll of quarters to back his knuckles, his fist impacting the man on the left side of the forehead, the eyes going wide, the body rolling, tumbling down, the right front wheel crushing the man's legs—but there was no scream, the blow to the head apparently having killed him.

Ten yards to go, the roar of the engine and the vibration louder, louder than Rourke had thought it could have been—he jumped clear as they hit five yards, the roar louder still as Rubenstein—Rourke glanced to the younger man as he jumped—hammered the gas pedal flat against the floor.

Rourke hit the ground, half rolling against a wildman, the wildman—tall, lean, the half-naked torso rippling with muscles under a fur poncho and cut-off jeans, lashing out with a Bowie bladed knife. Rourke's left fist groped for the second Detonics, found it, his left thumb passing behind the pistol's tang to work down the safety, then sweeping around as he fired the pistol point blank against the wildman's throat, blood bursting out of the wound in a wet sticky cloud as Rourke turned his

165

eyes away.

He pushed himself to his feet, hearing the grinding and tearing of metal, looking now toward the bunker doors, the outer door at least caved in.

Rourke started to run, hammering the empty pistol in his right fist against the face of a woman with a revolver, knocking her down, splitting her nose down the center, her scream shrill, agonized as he ran on. A wildman from his left—Rourke fired the second Detonics, a two-round burst into the chest, the man toppling back.

Rourke was beside the truck, Rubenstein visible through the still open right side door, sprawled across the seat.

"Paul!"

The younger man looked up. "All right—okay —I'm all right."

Rourke punched the Detonics pistol in his left fist forward. "Down!" He fired three times, emptying the pistol, mutilating the face of the wildman with the butcher knife starting for Paul through the sprung-open driver's side door.

Rubenstein rolled against the seat back, pushing up the CAR-15, firing through the open door behind him as more of the wildmen rushed the truck.

Rourke, both pistols empty, wheeled, a short, stocky man wearing animal skins and blue jeans hurtling his body toward him.

Rourke took its full force, sprawling back against the side of the bunker, the concrete rough and hard against the skin of his neck as he slipped down along its length, the man going for his throat. Rourke found his knife with his left hand, dropping

166

the Detonics to the ground, his right arm pinned at his side, his left hand arcing forward and around, driving the knife in under the right rib cage—there was a scream, a curse, the body slumping away for an instant, Rourke's right arm free, his right fist hammering down with the Detonics, the butt crushing into the face of the wildman, smashing the nose, as Rourke's left knee slammed upward, smashing into the groin.

Rourke sidestepped as the body fell, the second pistol still on the ground, buttoning out the magazine in the pistol in his right hand, catching the empty and ramming home a fresh one from the six pack. His right thumb worked down the slide stop, his first finger pulling the trigger, killing a wildman lunging at him with a spear.

Rourke slumped back against the concrete wall for an instant, inhaling hard—

He reached across the body of the man he'd knifed, found his second pistol, reloaded it, then found his knife—he had emptied the Sparks six pack and had only the remaining magazines in his musette bag and on his belt—

"John—inside!"

Rourke looked to his right—Rubenstein and O'Neal were gone, the door to the bunker pried partially away from the jamb.

He glanced skyward, Natalia in the helicopter making another pass over the ground—

Rourke threw himself up, over the hood of the truck, swinging his legs over and dropping down, firing the pistol in his right hand at a man with a spear as he hit the ground, then pushing himself through the space between the metal door and the jamb.

"Here!"

It was half in shadow in the narrow space behind the door and he felt a hand on his left forearm. "Me, John!"

Through the crack between the door and the jamb, Rourke could see wildmen massing for an assault against the door, the one called Otis, blood oozing through his fingers as he held his shoulder, at their head.

Rourke looked behind him, his eyes gradually accustomed to the gloom. He ripped his sunglasses from his face, stuffing them into the inside pocket of his bomber jacket.

"Paul—you and O'Neal get as far back as you can go—hurry."

Rourke edged back, away from the door, the assault starting, the Detonics in his right hand coming up, in his mind's eye trying to judge the perfect spot for hitting the fuel pump—he fired, throwing himself back, the truck roaring into an explosion, Rourke suddenly gasping for air as he looked back, the heat of the explosion making a wind, sucking air from inside the bunker. Rourke coughed, lurching forward on his hands, his fists still clenched on the twin Detonics pistols—there was screaming from outside.

Rourke pushed himself to his feet and half threw himself into the deeper shadow ahead, down the tunnel leading into the main body of the bunker.

Cole would be arming the missiles to launch— and millions would die.

Chapter Thirty-Five

Rourke raced ahead, leaving Rubenstein and O'Neal beside the second door—the one with the combination lock, wide open—if Cole had closed it, Rourke would have been powerless to stop him. Rourke ran on, lights gleaming in the corners where the low concrete ceiling met the walls, such little room in the passage that if Rourke jogged slightly left or right, his shoulders would brush against the walls.

He could hear the humming of machinery—generators working—the lighting and the missiles-firing devices were all on the same electrical system, he assumed.

He could see brighter light at the far edge of the tunnel and he threw himself more into the run, his arms at his sides, his pistols clutched in both fists—he would kill Cole in cold blood if he had to to stop him.

The end of the passage was less than twenty yards away, Rourke cocking his head back, his mouth wide open gulping at the stale, cool air, Rourke skidding on his combat boot heels across the last yard or so, lurching against the door frame—the missile control room.

Cole—leaning across a panel of switches and lights, computer tapes whirring.

Rourke shouted, "Cole—don't!"

Cole turned, his face a snarl, his lips drawn back across his uneven teeth, his eyes glinting, the front of his body covered in mud-smeared blood. "For America!"

Cole threw himself across the panel nearest him, both pistols in Rourke's fists bucking and bucking again and again, the noise deafening, his ears ringing, Cole's body sliding down from the panel, his left arm extended.

Rourke saw it—as if in slow motion—the push of a button, a red button.

The lighting in the control room switched from whitish yellow to a dull red, a mechanical voice booming over a speaker near Rourke's head, his ears still ringing from the concentrated gunfire in the confined space.

Cole's body fell to the floor, rolled, the eyes blank and staring upward.

The computer voice announced, "T minus ten minutes and counting—irretrievable launch sequence initiated. T minus nine minutes forty-five seconds and counting."

Rourke stared at the speaker. "Shit."

Chapter Thirty-Six

Rourke whirled the dials on the radio—praying the electromagnetic pulse hadn't reached this far into the ground, the electromagnetic pulse that had wiped out the air base communications until Teal—the late Armand Teal—had jerry-rigged to restore them.

"Calling the helicopter—Natalia! Come in, damnit!"

"John—where are—"

"No time—in the bunker—launch is—" the mechanical voice again—"T minus eight minutes fifty seconds and counting"—"You hear that?"

"Yes—yes—"

"Get down here—I'm going into the silos—try to disarm the electrical system that would trigger the launch—the panel here is armor plated and I can't get into it. Follow me—we've gotta try—Rourke out!" Rourke threw down the microphone, both Detonics pistols already holstered, his hands at his sides as he ran for the metal steps leading down toward the silo maintenance access tunnel just ahead.

He ran—he prayed.

Chapter Thirty-Seven

Natalia shouted to the machine gunner, "I'm taking her down, seaman—I have to get inside the bunker and help Dr. Rourke!"

"Yes, ma'am!"

She made the helicopter rotate a full three hundred sixty degrees as she scanned the ground for a safe place to land—there was none. She picked a spot within two hundred yards or so of the bunker entrance and the still-burning truck at the door—she started down. "Hang on," she sang out.

The landing party forces were consolidating to complete the envelopment. The wildmen, perhaps a hundred of them still—fighting hand to hand with the landing party forces now, gunfire pouring from a knot of the wildmen near the bunker doors, into the bunker itself, as best she could discern.

She jockeyed the controls, the helicopter touching down. She killed her engine for the tail rotor, then the main rotor, and pressed the quick release button of her seat restraint harness, jumping out and to the ground, snatching up her M-16.

Wildmen were everywhere—and she had to get to the bunker.

"Hey, ma'am—this'll help ya!"

She looked behind her—it was the gunner with the machine gun detached from its mounts, the link belt draped across his body as he framed himself into the doorway. The machine gun began to spit tongues of flame into the mass of wildmen.

Natalia shot him a wave, then started to run.

She shouted to the shore party men—"Follow me—to the bunker—I have to get inside! Follow me!"

The men began to rally around her, forming a wedge with her at its center as she ran, pumping the trigger of her M-16, cutting down each target of opportunity, men and women, headshots, shots to the chest, bursts that ripped away the nameless faces—she kept running.

The M-16 came up dry and she rammed the butt of the weapon against the face of a wildman with a spear—his nose crushed under its impact as he fell back and away from her.

She threw the rifle at another of the wildmen, snatching open the holster flaps and drawing her L-Frame stainless Smiths, the ones customized by Ron Mahovsky for Sam Chambers before his ascendancy to the presidency of U.S. II, the ones he had given her as a gesture of friendship for her aid in the evacuation of peninsular Florida, the ones with the American eagles on the barrel flats—she fired both .357 Magnums at once, putting two slugs into the chest of a wildman coming at her with an assault rifle blazing—she ran on.

They were nearing the doorway into the bunker, the truck still smoldering but some of the wildmen—a man in Levis and a bearskin their apparent leader—creeping around the sides of the truck, gunfire coming from inside the bunker—it would be Paul and O'Neal, she realized.

They ran ahead. "Get that squat man with the bearskin—he must be the leader," she shouted.

The wildmen near the bunker door turned now, almost as one, raining their assault rifles, firing them out in long, ragged bursts, Natalia seeing some of the men from the shore party going down, Natalia's guns blazing in her hands, gunfire from both sides of her from the shore party, the wildmen going down as well.

Both revolvers were empty and she rammed them into her holsters, securing the flaps, bending down, snatching up an M-16 from the ground beside her, standing then, firing out the rifle into the wildmen.

"Close with them!" She started to run, using the rifle alternately like a spear and a club, ramming the flash deflector into a face, swatting the stock against a head, butting the stock against a rib cage.

She stopped—a half dozen of the wildmen in a knot around the squat man who was their leader. The shore party men were around her.

Natalia threw the rifle to the ground, reaching into her hip pocket for the Bali-Song knife, her thumb flicking up the lock that bound the two skeletonized handle sections together, then the interior of the right thumb joint sliding into the open depression in the rear handle section, the knife held between her thumb joint and the side of her first finger, the forward section and the blade rocking forward, the second finger of her right hand forming a fulcrum under the near handle half, and she rocked the near handle half down, both handle halves swinging together, her fist locking around them.

She pressured the near handle half, the Wee-Hawk blade edge outward—with her thumb and first finger, flicking her wrist, rolling her hand and closing the knife, repeating the same motion, but finishing the circle and rolling the knife inward to open it again.

She advanced toward the squat wildman with the bearskin wrapped around him, a knife the size of a short sword appeared in his blood-covered right hand.

He lunged, Natalia feigned, backed off a half-step and rolled the knife closed, then open, lunging as she rolled the knife closed again, then open again, lunging and parrying as she closed the knife, then rolled it open, the man with the bearskin lunging, her blade open, her fist clenched tight around it, her right arm punching out, the Wee-Hawk blade's tip punching into the carotid artery on the right side of the neck, ripping, tearing—the man fell away, dead.

Natalia did another roll of the knife, closed and open, then leaned down, smearing the blade clean of blood against the bearskin, then rolling it closed and turning the knife end over end in her fist, then closing the lock shut. She dropped it in her hip pocket, the others of the wildmen dead around her, some of the shore party still standing beside her, gunfire from near the helicopter, but mostly the fire from the M-60 machine gun being used.

"Paul—it is Natalia—I must get inside!"

176

She glanced at the gold lady's Rolex on her left wrist—she judged perhaps five minutes remained until launch.

And if she and Rourke were in the access tunnel trying to confuse or disarm the system when the first missile hit ignition—they would be vaporized.

"Paul!"

"Come ahead, Natalia!"

Again, she started to run.

Chapter Thirty-Eight

Rourke used the small stainless steel screwdriver on his key ring to remove the last of the bolts over what he hoped was the master electrical panel cover. He tugged at the ends—it was jammed. He withdrew the Black Chrome Sting IA from its sheath, using it to pry against the cover—the cover snapped loudly, echoing in the tunnel as the mechanical voice droned on—"T minus five minutes twenty-five seconds and counting—T minus five minutes twenty-seconds and counting—T minus five minutes fifteen seconds and counting."

"Shut up!" he shouted. "Shut up, damnit!"

"T minus five minutes five seconds and counting," the voice almost answered.

Beneath the panel were a maze of multicolored wires—he had wired his own home, wired the Retreat—he had wired bombs of conventional explosives—he had never seen such a confusing array of wires in his life. Some would be blinds, some double blinds, some trip detonators that would fuse all the wires in the panel and make disarming the system totally impossible—"Shit," he rasped.

Rourke glanced to his left—"T minus four minutes fifty seconds and counting.''

He could see the fin section of the nearest of the missiles, this the missile that would launch first, its flame discharge sufficient to vaporize him before he would have the chance to realize it was happening.

''T minus four minutes forty seconds and counting.''

''Shut up—''

Rourke snatched one of the Detonics pistols out of the double Alessi rig and fired up into the speaker box at the far end of the tunnel.

But still he could hear the voice, only more distant from the next farther speaker.

''T minus four minutes thirty five seconds and counting.''

Rourke holstered his gun, studying the wiring diagram—''Come on, Natalia—damnit—come on!'' She knew the system better than he did—had studied its stolen plans. For once in his life he prayed Soviet Intelligence had gotten perfect information.

Rourke touched at the nearest blue wire—he followed it out to the terminal—his hands gloved to guard against electrocution—but leather wouldn't do much he knew—he worked with his tiny screwdriver.

The computer voice droned on. ''T minus four minutes twenty seconds and counting.''

Didn't the voice know that it too would die, he thought?

Chapter Thirty-Nine

"T minus four minutes, fifteen seconds and counting." Natalia heard the voice, stared for a moment at Cole's dead eyes, then ran on, her pistol holsters slapping at her sides, her feet seeming to her barely to touch the concrete floor as she reached the ladder, then started down three rungs at a time to the lower level and to the missile access tunnel. "T minus four minutes five seconds and counting."

The voice was maddening. . . .

Rourke looked up, hearing the thudding of heels on the concrete. "T minus three minutes twenty seconds and counting. T minus three minutes fifteen seconds and counting. T minus three minutes ten seconds and counting. T minus three minutes five seconds and counting. T minus three minutes to irretrievable launch. Two minutes fifty-five seconds to launch. T minus two minutes fifty seconds and counting."

Natalia—he shouted her name—"Natalia!"

She skidded on her heels, dropping into a crouch beside him at the electrical panel—six wires were removed, three cut—he held his knife against a fourth, his finger behind the wire.

"What happened when you cut these?" she said breathlessly.

"Nothing—not a damn thing—"

"This could take hours and we still might fuse the wires and automatically trigger a launch—"

"Shit," he rasped.

"I love you, John—I think we're going to die here—"

"I love you, too," he told her, the knife blade still poised over the wire.

"Don't cut that—I wish we'd had more time together—I wish you'd made love to me—"

"I couldn't—why shouldn't I cut it—"

"Sarah could never understand how lucky she is—that you love her—were faithful to her—"

"I had no choice—it's me—it wasn't you—it's the way I'm made—I wanted to so much—"

She looked at him, Rourke taking her hand, squeezing it. "I never loved anyone like I love you," he whispered.

"I'll love you even after death—"

"T minus two minutes five seconds and counting. T minus two minutes and counting."

"The wires have to be the way to stop this," Rourke rasped.

She shifted her gaze, Rourke following it as she picked up the cover panel that had been over the wiring itself.

"That protected the wires—"

"Protected—" She dropped the panel, threw her arms around his neck and kissed him, Rourke feeling her mouth full against his lips. Breathless, she told him, "That's it—if I can find the preignition

182

wire here, I can activate the ignition test sequence and start the nearest of the missiles to burn—''

"What are you talking about—''

"The panel, John—that's what it did—the packing inside—all around here—fireproof—it's like a fireproof vault—these launch in series—these missiles. If the panel and the circuit box weren't fireproofed, the first burn would destroy the launch system wiring and the other five missiles wouldn't launch at all—if I can get an ignition check burn, the flames will vaporize the wiring and the system will be dead—''

"So will we,'' Rourke added. "What do we do—''

"Maybe not—I can rig a delay—maybe fifteen seconds just by stripping away most of the insulation on one of the wires and grounding it to a hot wire—say for the lights—''

"If you know what you're talking about, fine— you lost me—do it.''

"You run—I'll do it myself.''

"T minus one minute thirty-five seconds and counting. T minus one minute thirty seconds and counting.'' A claxxon began to sound, the computer voice louder now to be heard over it. "T minus one minute twenty-five seconds and counting.''

"I'll stay with you—I won't leave you—I won't.''

She looked at him—her eyes, their incredible blueness, her skin so white, her hair almost unnatural in its darkness, a lock of it fallen across her forehead, her left hand unconsciously brushing it back from her face.

183

"Take my gloves—"

"I have my own—tighter fit," she nodded, smiling.

"T minus one minute fifteen seconds and counting."

Natalia began tracing out wires with her right hand, Rourke helping her into the left skintight leather glove. She took the right glove, pulling it on herself as he watched her eyes follow out the wiring system.

"I have no way of knowing if this is the right wire—I think it is—but I don't know—"

"T minus one minute five seconds and counting. T minus one minute to irretrievable launch ignition—preignition in ten seconds. T minus forty-five seconds."

"That's it—their preignition burn—I can get it here—"

"T minus forty seconds—"

Her hands moved across the panel, a wire ripped free, the Bali-Song coming out in her right hand, the blade a blur of gleaming steel, the blade slicing against the plastic coating of a blue wire.

"Preignition burn—"

Natalia fell back, screaming—"John—"

Rourke grabbed her in his arms and felt the electrical current pulse through her, throwing his weight and hers away from the panel and ripping her free.

She was breathing—barely.

The computer voice droned. "T minus twenty-five seconds. T minus twenty—"

The voice was swallowed in the roar of the missile engine.

Rourke, his body trembling still from the electrical shock, pushed himself to his feet, his hands clawing Natalia's body to his chest, his right shoulder butting into her abdomen as he flung her across it, the roar of the engine deafening now.

A glance behind him—a ball of flame rolling from the nearest of the missiles.

Rourke started to run—

The claxxon still sounded, louder than before, the roar of the fireball behind him, the heat oppressive—his lungs ached, his chest ached.

"No, I won't die!" He screamed the words to the tunnel walls around him as he ran, an explosion from behind him, the electrical conduit along the tunnel ceiling afire now, the lights—fluorescent tubes—bursting, exploding, flecks of razor-sharp glass raining down on him as he ran.

The fireball—he could smell it, taste it; he stole a glance over his shoulder as he ran—it was blindingly bright and right behind him.

Ahead, he could see the door to the access tunnel entrance—Natalia had left it ajar as had he—he opened his mouth wide, the hot burning air seeming to sear his lungs as he gulped it to sustain him—he ran.

The door was twenty yards away—he couldn't remember if it was fireproof—fifteen yards away. Ten yards. He glanced behind him, the fireball nearer, his left foot buckling, but he caught his balance. Five yards. Rourke threw himself through the doorway, lurching and twisting, hurtling his weight against the door, slamming it, his left hand snaking out to the bolt latch—his fingers burning as he touched it.

The door was starting to melt.

Rourke kept running—ahead—perhaps fifty yards ahead was the access ladder to the control room.

"John—" The cough—the voice—Natalia.

Rourke slowed, leaning his weight against the wall as he stopped, slipping Natalia to her feet—"What—"

"Fireball—other—other side—the door—melting—"

As if punctuating his words, there was a groaning sound, then the roar of the fireball—the door was gone.

"Run for it," and Rourke shoved her ahead, Natalia starting to run, outdistancing him, fresher—Rourke ran, picking up his feet, laying them down, shouting to himself internally—"Run!"

Twenty-five yards to the ladder now. Twenty—the conduit overhead here was afire as well, Rourke feeling the heat searing at the exposed skin on the back of his neck, the roar of the fireball so loud he could no longer even hear his own labored breathing.

Ten yards. Five.

Natalia was up the ladder, two rungs at a time.

Rourke threw himself against it—Natalia's hands were reaching down—there was no time, no sense —to argue. He took her hands, Natalia half pulling him up the ladder. He stumbled forward, after her, jumping over Cole's body, Natalia ahead of him, shouting, breathless—"Paul—get out of here—run for it!"

Rourke stumbled, caught himself against the

wall—the concrete seemed burning hot to the touch.

He kept running, Natalia was ahead of him, daylight there, the fluorescent tubes on the tunnel sides exploding still, the conduit itself making a sheet of flames above their heads, the fireball being sucked faster, he knew—toward the oxygen.

The doorway—five yards. Two yards. Natalia was through, Rourke throwing himself through and past the burnt truck and behind her, running, throwing himself to the ground and right, the fireball belching out as he rolled, his hands going to protect his face.

Then it was gone. No missile contrails were in the air as he moved his hands from his face.

He didn't know how long it was—he was too tired to look at his watch.

But after a time—she was crawling toward him on her knees, then slumped against him, he heard Natalia's voice, felt her hands touch at the back of his neck—he was sore there, tender.

"You have the worst sunburn I've ever seen," she laughed.

Rourke put his arms around her and held her body close against him.

He closed his eyes.

Chapter Forty

"As best I can make out," O'Neal smiled, rubbing his dirty hands across his dirty, soot-smeared face, "when that fireball hit the air out here it got hot enough to melt down everything that wasn't concrete—that tunnel is sealed tighter than a drum and there wasn't a cookoff—no radiation at all. We lucked out—or I should say you did."

Rourke looked up at him. Rourke squatted on the ground, Natalia behind him rubbing a cream into the burn on his neck. "We can put a charge over that mound along the ridge there and bury the missile bunker entrance completely—what about an earthquake someday here?"

"Well, maybe—"

"Unless a fault was created on the Night of The War, they wouldn't have built this anywhere near one—it should be safe forever."

"Maybe somebody a thousand years from now will dig it up—"

"Perhaps someone a thousand years from now will be too smart to want to," Rourke heard Natalia murmur from behind him.

"A shame our people and your people couldn't

have worked together—well, like we did here—before—well, before all—"

"Before the Night of The War," Paul Rubenstein added somberly, his jacket and shirt gone, his left arm and shoulder heavily bandaged, his eyes glassy from the painkiller Rourke had given him before cleaning and dressing the wound.

"Maybe someday," O'Neal said, squinting against the afternoon sun—Rourke was reminded to find his glasses in his bomber jacket pocket—"somebody'll remember what this place was—maybe build a little marker here, you know?"

Thunder rumbled out of the cloudless sky, the sun blood-red.

"Maybe someday," Rourke almost whispered. "Maybe."

Chapter Forty-One

Bill Mulliner realized two things—one was he was more frightened than he had ever been in his life because, since the successful raid on the supply depot in Nashville and the theft of arms, ammunition, and medical supplies, Russian troops were everywhere. The other thing he felt was pride—his father had died in an abortive attempt at a similar raid—the success now in at least a small way avenging his father's death.

His father—he still hadn't, he realized, adjusted to the idea of his father's not being there. The scratchy beard stubble when he hadn't shaved—despite Bill's age, he would kiss his father on the cheek. The warm, sweatiness of the man's skin, the dry firmness though of his hand when it had clasped his.

The man he could talk to, not always well, but talk to—this was gone from him forever, and as he walked, three M-16s slung on his shoulders and one eight-hundred-round can of 5.56mm ammo in each hand, he cried.

But only the darkness of the forest could see him—Pete Critchfield and the others walked far ahead. . . .

Sarah Rourke looked up from the injured black man whose bandage she had just changed, the man's eyes wide in the darkness as he too had heard the sound. She had the Trapper .45 in her right hand, thumbing back the hammer.

"What is it?" Mary Mulliner whispered hoarsely.

Sarah heard Michael make the sound, "Shh."

Annie, who had helped her with the injured man's bandage—mainly making him smile—clutched her left arm.

"Mrs. Rourke?"

It was Bill Mulliner's voice, beside him, slightly ahead of him coming into the clearing, Pete Critchfield—before he reached the edge of the sheltered fire on which she boiled water, she could smell the fetid smoke of his cigar.

"Bill—Pete—how'd it—"

"Lost two men—and Jim Hastings and Curly got the rest with them, stashing the loot—"

"You make yourself sound like a criminal for stealing American supplies from the Russians—don't call it loot, Pete," she said hastily.

"All right—the stuff, then—weapons, ammunition, explosives, some medical supplies—I'm carrying the medical stuff and some explosives—Bill here's got the ammo and Tom—you donno Tom—he's got more of the medical stuff for ya."

The third man nodded. "Ma'am."

"Tom," she nodded back—he was black, like the man she treated now.

"Left two men up by the road," Critchfield went on—"Russians ever'where now—"

"You must have made a big splash," she smiled, her voice low.

"Yeah, well—destroyed an ammo truck, killed about eighteen or nineteen of their people, took what we could pack in a van we stole and blew up the rest—I'd say they was a might flustered, leastways."

And Critchfield laughed, Sarah hearing the man on the ground beside her laugh too and say, "You fight near as good as us black folks, Pete!"

Sarah looked at her patient, then ran her left hand across his head, telling him, "You rest easy—so you can laugh later."

Mary Mulliner—Sarah guessed she liked none of it—said, "I'll make you men some coffee."

Somehow, Sarah thought, there was an odd sound in Bill Mulliner's voice. "Okay, Mom." His face looked worn and afraid, somehow older than Sarah had ever seen it. . . .

"If they got David Balfry alive," Pete Critchfield said, warming his hands on his coffee cup as he looked at her, "then they'll like as not get David to talk—tell 'em ever'thing he knows 'bout the Resistance. And he knows a lot, he does."

"God bless him," Sarah whispered.

"Amen," Mary Mulliner added.

"Mommie—hold me—I'm cold," Annie pleaded, Sarah folding her left arm around the child, picking up her coffee cup in her right hand.

"Could we try to bust him out?" Bill asked suddenly, blurting it out, his blue eyes wide in the firelight, the pupils like pinpoints, his red hair across his forehead.

"David—outa Chicago? That's where they'd take him—no. Can't. David's done—simple as that. And he'd be wantin' us to think that, too. Write him off 'stead of gettin' ourselves killed tryin' to bust him outa there. Probably use drugs to get him to talk. No—I figure we gotta go on—that's what David'd be wantin' us to do. I gotta contact U.S. II headquarters—talk with that Reed fella in Intelligence—see if'n he knows what the Russians is about with all these supplies and things. There's a farm—not far from your old place, Mrs. Mulliner— the Cunningham place. Raised quarter horses before The War—beautiful things. But old Mr. Cunningham was a ham radio operator. Still got all his equipment. We never used the place, kept it on the back burner, so to speak, for a safe house, like they call it in the spy movies. Well—we're usin' it now— and that radio—"

"The Cunninghams are dead—a raid—" Bill Mulliner began.

"Brigands?" Michael asked.

"Brigands," Critchfield nodded. "But them Brigands burned the house and the barns—old Cunningham had him a machine shop underground of the house—kind of a survivalist like Mrs. Rourke's husband was—"

"Is," Sarah corrected unconsciously.

"Yes, Sarah—is," Critchfield nodded. "Cunningham and his missus got killed fighting the Brigands—but the underground part never got touched. All we gotta do is rig up some sorta antenna like and use that ham radio of his. Food and some ammo stored there, too. Can make it there in about six hours hard walkin' time."

"Then let's go," Sarah said. "Most of my wounded can walk all right—we can stretcher carry the one that can't—both legs shot up, but he's still strong."

"Then it's agreed?" Critchfield nodded.

"Agreed," Bill Mulliner added.

"Agreed," Annie laughed, and everyone laughed with her—except Sarah. She thought of David Balfry—he had kissed her. And now he would be enduring something she didn't even want to imagine.

"Agreed," Sarah finally said.

There were Russians everywhere, and if they made it to the Cunningham place unmolested, it would be a miracle. And there were Brigands, too—she felt almost evil thinking it, but perhaps the Russians and the Brigands would lock horns and just kill each other and make it all over, all done with. Perhaps.

She sipped at her coffee and it was cold and bitter to taste.

Chapter Forty-Two

General Ishmael Varakov heard the clicking of heels on the museum floor—he knew, without looking up from his file-folder-littered desk that it would be Rozhdestvenskiy, come with absurd punctuality for his appointment.

The clicking of heels neared as Varakov studied the urgent communique from the Kremlin leadership still in hiding in their bunker. "Rozhdestvenskiy and the KGB are to be given full aid and support of the army, the GRU and any other forces or facilities at your command. The Womb is the ultimate priority project—this is to be given your full efforts." It was signed by the Central Committee and The People of The Soviet.

Varakov smiled—was that like SPQR—Senatus Populusque Romanus? He remembered what had happened to them.

"Comrade General!"

There was a louder click of heels, and Varakov still studied the communique.

Without looking up, he murmured, "Sit down, colonel—it appears I am ordered to assist you and this Womb Project. But as commanding general still

197

I must first insist that I be informed as to the total implications of my orders—"

"Comrade General—"

Varakov looked up, Rozhdestvenskiy—blonde, athletic, firm-jawed, handsome by any standard, erect even when sitting—again the image of the SS officer came to Varakov's mind.

"Yes, colonel?"

"All work with factories for prosecuting The War effort with The People's Republic of China and remaining NATO troops is to be temporarily put aside. All agricultural production not vital to the Womb effort is to be put aside—all energies, as your orders indicate, are to be devoted to the speedy development of the Womb Project to its ultimate goal."

"What is this ultimate goal, colonel—" Varakov would not call him comrade—those he had called comrade had meant too much to him to so debase, so abuse the word.

He watched Rozhdestvenskiy—not a hair out of place, the uniform neat, perfect, without a wrinkle—so unlike his own, which even he realized much of the time looked as though it was slept in. It was.

"In simple terms, Comrade General—"

"Yes—we must be simple—"

"There was no slight meant to you, Comrade General—I have always held the deepest admiration for your past distinguished military career—"

"Please—spare me—"

Rozhdestvenskiy raised his right eyebrow, his lips downturned at the corners, held tight together, his eyes seeming to emit a light of their own. "Very well—the goal of the Womb is much the same as the goal of the American Eden Project—the survival of the best and finest ideology. But we shall triumph—the Americans will not—"

"You speak in hyperbole, colonel—be more concrete."

"The Eden Project was conceived to ensure the survival of the Western Democracies at all costs in the event of a global nuclear confrontation. The Womb will counter this last desperate gesture of the degenerate Capitalist system, and at once ensure the eternal triumph and majesty of the People's Revolution. But one element is missing, one needed element. To accomplish this goal, to ensure the very survival of the Soviet system, of Communism itself, the military must be fully committed to release KGB-attached forces to pursue that needed element, without which the Womb is doomed and American Imperialism will triumph."

"And what about the survival of the Soviet people, colonel?" Varakov asked, his voice sounding dull to him. "What of their survival?"

Rozhdestvenskiy smiled. "May I be blunt, Comrade General?"

"A change, yes."

"The spirit of the Soviet people, of the struggling masses everywhere, is best embodied in the political leadership of the Soviet and in the KGB as its extension of will—"

"And the people be damned," Varakov said flatly, staring at Rozhdestvenskiy.

"The sheer force of numbers implies at its most

199

basic conceptualization arbitrary selection—"

"An ark—like Noah in the Judeo Christian Bible—but an ark by invitation only, based on dialectics?"

"You do know—all of it," Rozhdestvenskiy almost whispered.

"I do know—all of it—"

"There will be room for you, Comrade General—"

Varakov laughed. "I have lived long enough to sleep for five hundred years—to awaken to what?"

"Perhaps your niece if she can be found—"

"To be your concubine—or to be executed because you consider her to have had complicity in the death of Karamatsov—hardly, colonel."

"You have been ordered by Moscow—"

"I have been ordered by what was Moscow—and is now a group of old men afraid to die with dignity because they did not live with dignity—old men who hide in a bunker and are so afraid, so distrusting, that not even their commanding generals know exactly where the bunker is located. Are they packed—and waiting?"

"Yes, Comrade General—"

"Do not call me comrade—I have been given orders. I have spent my entire life since I was fifteen obeying military orders. Now I am reduced to obeying the orders of cowardly murderers who save themselves over the finest of Soviet youth—I will follow the letter of my orders—have your troops— have them all. But I am not your comrade—I have never been—you are dismissed, colonel."

Varakov looked from the eyes to his desk, studying the communique. He heard the chair move slightly as Rozhdestvenskiy would have stood up, heard the click of heels as Rozhdestvenskiy would have saluted, then the long pause when he—Varakov—did not look up to return the salute.

Finally, he heard the sound of heels on the floor of his place, his special place, the sound diminishing with each step.

There would not be a recall to Moscow, a premature pension—or perhaps an accident.

There would not be the time for that. He—Varakov—would die like all the rest.

His feet hurt badly.

Chapter Forty-Three

David Balfry opened his eyes—they hurt to open, his nose stiff and he could not breathe through it. The lights were bright.

He looked down to his chest, then looked away, sickened, the nipples of his breasts black, burned, the electrodes still clipped to them.

"You are awake?" The voice was almost kind-sounding. "He is awake—let us be sure—"

Balfry felt the pain starting in his testicles—the burning, felt it, smelled his flesh as it smoked. "No-o-o-o-o—-Christ, no—!"

The pain stopped and he was numb except for a core of pain still somewhere inside the pit of his stomach.

"Then you will cooperate and tell us the information we request about the so-called Resistance?" There was a laugh.

"Fuck you," Balfry stammered, his tongue thick-feeling, his words strange-sounding to him— his teeth gone, broken, his tongue swollen from thirst, cut where it scraped against the jagged edge of his teeth. They had used a hammer and chisel part of the time—part of the time pliers. The salty taste started again in his houth and he knew he was bleeding.

"Our dental care—our electrical stimulation—you found this offensive? Hmm." The voice—he could not see the face—cooed to him. "Hard on you? Painful, even?" There was laughter in the frightening darkness beyond the light. "There are things unspeakable in yours or any language—things we can make you endure, Balfry—but there are drugs to calm your pain, to ease you happily into death—these choices are yours to make. We have hours, days, weeks—as long as necessary."

"No, ya don't," Balfry coughed. "You need what I know—and you need it now—but to get it now you're gonna have to kill me—and then you won't have it—eat shit."

"A college professor—such a way for a university don to speak—let's try the electrodes to the breasts again—the twitching is interesting to watch."

The pain—it flooded his chest and he cried and felt ashamed. But he didn't talk—he would have laughed. With the pain, he couldn't talk.

Chapter Forty-Four

Rozhdestvenskiy entered the room at the far corner of the museum basement. What he saw made his stomach churn.

"You are barbarians—and worse than that—incompetent! This is an important prisoner whose information may be vital and you so risk his life!"

He couldn't see the face in the darkness beyond the light—all he could see was the captured Resistance leader, Balfry.

"But, Comrade Colonel!"

He recognized the voice—and more than that, his eyes drifting across the naked, horribly abused body strapped against the "work" table, the table hanging the man almost completely inverted—the technique.

"You will call medical assistance immediately—the man will be treated, made comfortable and then administered drugs—drugs against which he can offer no resistance and that will allow his successful interrogation—not this butchery.

"You are insane—" and Rozhdestvenskiy started out the door—

"Comrade Colonel—"

Rozhdestvenskiy, his hand on the knob, stopped, not turning back, not wanting to see the American again.

"He is dead, Comrade Colonel—I—I had no idea that—"

Rozhdestvenskiy leaned against the door, letting it slam closed under his weight.

"Have the man's body—what remains of it— given a decent burial. He is the equivalent of an enemy officer—he deserves such." And Rozhdestvenskiy turned, stepping quickly into the shadow, reaching out, his left hand finding the throat of the man whose technique he knew so well, hated so well.

"And if you ever—ever attempt such a thing again—when the time comes, rather than a long sleep and renewed life—I will disembowel you with greater zest than I have ever killed any other man—" Rozhdestvenskiy pushed the torturer away, heard the clatter of the body falling against what sounded like an instrument tray, upsetting it, over-turning it, metallic objects and glass tinkling against the stone flcor.

Rozhdestvenskiy stepped out of the shadow, walked back to the door and looked once again at the now dead American, Balfry.

"When one lives with animals," Rozhdestvenskiy began, never finishing, going out through the doorway and closing the memory behind him.

Chapter Forty-Five

The submarine's deck winch shifted, Rourke's Harley the last of the three bikes to be put onto the rocks. No dock, they had carefully explored a section of coastline, finding a flat rocky surface with deep enough soundings for the submarine to get within ten yards—Rourke standing now on the rock, salt spray blowing on the wind, Natalia and Paul Rubenstein already moving away along the spit of rock to the shore, only Commander Gundersen beside him now as the Jet Black Harley Low Rider swung precariously from the tackle, then was lowered slowly down.

"How's O'Neal?"

"Got him in sick bay—got a few more cuts and bruises during that bruha you folks had with Cole and the others. But he's just fine. Told me to give you his best regards—and to wish you luck finding your family."

"Tell him I wish him the same—the best of luck, and if he's looking for someone, to find them—and—well, tell him," Rourke added lamely.

Gundersen laughed. "All right—I'll tell him exactly that."

"Where you bound to?"

"Close as I can get this boat to U.S. II headquarters without a Russian reception committee to welcome me, I guess," Gundersen laughed.

"Then what?"

"Funny talk for a guy who rides around under water, but guess you could say I'm a quote-unquote soldier—I'll follow my orders. Finally got through to U.S. II—ran a radio link through a ham set opened up last night in Tennessee—some Resistance people just got onto it—fella named Critchfield. Know him?"

"No—he didn't mention anything about a woman and two children, did he?"

"No—can't say I asked, either, though—sorry about that."

"I'm heading there anyway, once I get back."

"Well—we made the link," Gundersen said. "Seems Cole was really Thomas Iversenn. Reed called him a kudzu commando?"

"Yeah—kudzu's a plant, imported from Japan years ago—grows worse than a weed in Georgia—it's a vine. Covers up telephone poles, abandoned houses—"

"Really?"

"Yeah—but what about Cole—or Iversenn?"

"He was a National Guard officer—a first lieutenant. Wandered in one day with about a dozen men or so and volunteered to go regular army. They took him. Reed never really trusted him—right-wing radical, he called him. U.S. II assigned the real Cole and six men to recover the warheads to use as a bargaining tool against the Soviet Union.

Somehow, Iversenn found out about it—killed Cole and his men, Reed almost bought it. He took Cole's orders and identity."

"How'd he know so much about the missiles?"

"Worked at the facility that built the warheads—apparently—least figures it this way—this Iversenn had been planning to get to the missiles someday even if there hadn't been a war—start his own preemptive strike against the Soviet Union and alert Washington to join in or get retaliated against. Crazy."

"Yeah—he was," Rourke nodded, reaching out to the Harley, starting to ease it around as the tackle lowered it.

Gundersen helped him.

"What about you, John—Reed said he'd like you back. Gave me the coordinates for the new U.S. II headquarters and—"

"I'll memorize the coordinates—just in case I ever need them. But I've got my family to look for—what I was doing before Cole or Iversenn shot Natalia and started this whole thing."

"I'll ask you a favor then—with the jet fighter you've got stashed—"

"An experimental fighter bomber."

"Yeah—well, I know things on the water and under it—I leave airplanes to other people." And Gundersen laughed.

"What's the favor?"

"You said you rigged the ammo dumps and everything at Filmore Air Force base to blow if anyone tampered with it."

"Natalia and Paul did—good job, I understand."

209

"This is direct from President Chambers. If the Russians should land forces out here, we don't want them having an airfield to use, or any U.S. materiel or planes. Could their people debug the stuff Major Tiemerovna and Mr. Rubenstein did?"

"Probably—if they were careful," Rourke answered.

"Then I've got one order for you—order from President Chambers, a request from me."

"I take requests—I don't take orders," Rourke answered softly, easing his bike down and balancing it on the stand.

"Fire a missile into that ammo dump or whatever you need to do—destroy the base completely. . . ."

Rourke looked at him, then back to the Harley, undoing the binding that held it to the tackle. "All right—I'll make a run on it on the way East. Might not be perfect, but I'll tear up the main runways and hit the ammo dump and arsenal."

"Agreed—I'll tell Reed that—we're talking again before I go under."

Rourke extended his right hand, Gundersen taking it.

"Good luck to you, commander—"

"You, too, John—maybe we'll see each other again sometime."

Thunder rumbled loudly in the clear morning sky. And Rourke didn't answer Gundersen.

Chapter Forty-Six

Pete Critchfield seemed to explode. "You what?"

"I didn't think—didn't catch the lady's last name—"

"Shithead!" Critchfield looked back at Sarah, saying, "Excuse me, ma'am—" then looked at Curley. "Didn't catch her name—moron! You get that submarine back and tell that Gundersen fella to tell Dr. John Rourke we got his wife and two children here all safe and sound and he can come and get 'em when he gets here."

"But—I can't—the sub won't open a frequency with me for another hour—"

"Then you goddamned well tell 'em then!"

Critchfield turned away walking across the underground shelter's main room, Sarah hearing the hum of the electric generator as Critchfield walked, watching his face.

She looked up from the wounded man she was attending. "My husband?"

"There was a radio communication from a U.S. nuclear submarine on the west coast—whatever the hell the west coast is—we made the link to U.S. II headquarters for this Commander Gundersen. Him and me—we talked a little—then I hadda go relieve Bill Mulliner on guard duty—left Curley there monitoring the link—you know how—well, maybe you don't—but radio communications like this is funny—change in the air currents or somethin'. And there was lots of static—maybe all that thunder in the skies all the time. Anyways—Curley there heard them talkin' about a Dr. John Rourke and two friends of his—some Russian woman who's on our side maybe a little or leastways helped them out and a fella named Paul—''

"A Russian woman and a man named Paul," Sarah nodded.

"Anyways—Curley there—the asshole—excuse me again, ma'am," Critchfield shrugged, his face reddening, "he didn't say nothin' about you and the children. But they'll be talkin' again in an hour—Curley says. Then maybe we can put you and your husband on the radio together and talk a bit—then he can come here and get ya.''

"John," Sarah said—to talk to John Rourke. How long had it been.

She couldn't talk now—she just nodded her head and botched the bandage on the man she was helping.

"You relax there, ma'am," Critchfield smiled suddenly as she looked up. "I gotta send Bill Mulliner off with some guys down into Georgia a ways—there's a Resistance group down there I gotta contact. U.S. II wants us to get a headcount of still operating groups and warn 'em Balfry maybe talked.''

"Yes," she nodded, the word all she could say.

212

"I'll have Bill run down and say good-bye."

She nodded, licking her lips—she tried the bandage again.

Chapter Forty-Seven

She sat with Bill Mulliner, on the steps leading into the underground shelter, the house above them in the light through the open hatchway burned, some timbers remaining that laced a shadow across Bill's face as he sat beside her, his eyes looking down.

"I'm glad for you, ma'am—you findin' your husband."

"I don't know if I'll know what to say—all those times we fought over his preparing for—well—his preoccupation with survivalism. He was right—I could have been with him in his Retreat if I'd ever let him tell me where it was—or take us there."

"But I'm glad for knowin' ya, Mrs. Rourke—powerful glad."

She hugged her left arm around the boy's shoulders. "And I'm glad for knowing you, Bill—without your strength—the children and I wouldn't have—"

"Seems like you do real good on your own, ma'am," he laughed, but the laughter hollow sounding to her.

"Well—well, appearances are one thing—but to

have a man to turn to—to know you were there these
last days—I—I don't know what I would have done
without you," and she kissed him, hard on the lips
like she would have kissed a man twice his age,
closer her own age. She turned her face away, feeling embarrassed slightly, wringing her hands together over her knees, her feet spread wide apart on
the steps below her, but her knees locked together
tight.

She heard Bill Mulliner breathing. "Ma'am—
hope I meet a girl again—and she's—ahh—she's
like you," and she turned to look at him but he was
standing up, running up the steps.

Sarah Rourke closed her eyes—tight, like her
knees were tight and her throat was tight. Tight.

Chapter Forty-Eight

They used an old pickup truck that worked four-wheel drive—sometimes anyway, Bill Mulliner had determined. They were near the border with Georgia and he knew the area where they were going. It wasn't far from the little town he'd gone to once with the church group—Helen. It had been a Swiss village—right there in Georgia. He smiled, thinking about it—about the girl in the church group who had held his hand when they'd walked through the shops there.

His hands held the steering wheel now—too tightly.

The Resistance group—they had a name he couldn't remember—was hiding in the wild area in what had been the park around Anna Ruby Falls—he'd gone there once when he was really little, his mother had told him, kissing him good-bye as he'd boarded the truck.

He didn't remember it.

The truck jarred, bounced—the road was mud-rutted and bad, the gravel and clay slippery as he tried to hold the steering to keep them on the road and out of the yawning ditches on each side.

There were better roads—modern highways. But there would be Russians on them.

Here there would only be Brigands—and there were usually fewer of them, fewer and less well-armed these days. They had run out of people to steal from, towns to loot, food and weapons to kill for.

They wandered the countryside—sometimes heavily armed—but sometimes like scavengers. Kings once, they had thought themselves to be, he considered.

Now like lepers.

But dangerous lepers still—he watched the trees as did the man beside him in the cab and the men in the open bed of the truck behind the cab.

He could see their eyes, the leaness, the intensity their stares gave to their features as they watched the woods. Life would never be the same again, he suddenly thought.

Chapter Forty-Nine

Commander Gundersen leaned against the radio, wanted to hammer his fist against it. He didn't. If the radio broke he wouldn't be able to contact U.S. II.

"They are there—with you?" He said it into the microphone, not bothering with pro-words, call signs. He was too angry, too saddened for that.

"This is Undergrounder—affirmative on that, Bathtub."

The idiocy of the words they used—it amazed him. The idiocy of the entire thing.

By now, Rourke would be aboard his plane—the radio from the submarine wouldn't reach him— Rourke would keep the radio off to avoid Soviet detection. "Shit," Gundersen rasped, turning away from the set.

"Sir—what'll I—"

Gundersen looked behind him at the radio operator.

"Tell 'em—tell Mrs. Rourke--Jesus Christ, what'll I tell Mrs. Rourke?"

He stood there, balling his fists. In his mind, he said, "Mrs. Rourke—see, your husband left almost an hour ago. If he isn't at the plane by now, well—he will be soon and there's no way to reach him. He's planning to look around Tennessee—just stay there and maybe he'll find you—isn't that big a state, is it—Tennessee?''

He shook his head.

''Sir—what'll I—''

''Tell Mrs. Rourke that—ohh, Christ—I'll tell her—''

Gundersen picked up the microphone, then set it down again for an instant.

He didn't know what to say at all.

Chapter Fifty

General Ishmael Varakov sat in his seat behind his littered desk in his office without walls, the only face left for him to see without disgust that of Catherine.

He looked up, calling out across the museum hall to her. "Catherine!" He called again. "Catherine!"

He looked back to his desk, his papers—no word of Rourke, no word of his niece.

In seven to ten days—perhaps far less—it would all be done. Soon, very soon, finding them would only prove useless.

"Catherine!"

He looked up and she stood in front of his desk.

"Comrade General!"

He sighed, loudly, his feet hurting. He stood up, stuffing his feet as best he could into his shoes.

"You have a mother who lives?"

"Yes, Comrade General—on a collective farm near Minsk."

"I am ordering her transported—to a villa I own on the Black Sea—it is still beautiful there. See to it that the orders are written. And you have a brother?''

"Yes, Comrade General—he fights with our forces in northern Italy, I think.''

"Send my orders to his commanding general—I outrank the man. Your brother is ordered to my villa on the Black Sea as well.''

"But—but, Comrade General, I—''

He walked—the effort great because he was very tired. He passed around the desk, taking Catherine's hands in his, taking the notebook and pencil from her.

"We are all going to die—you should be with the ones you love at this time, Catherine, and you will issue my orders for your transportation as well—this is top priority. You will want for nothing there. You will be with the ones you love.''

Her eyes—wet, tearing, looked up into his. "I will issue the orders for my mother, Comrade General—and for my brother. To be together. I will not issue the orders for my own transportation.''

"You are loyal, child—but you must be with the ones you love, now.''

"I will stay here, Comrade General,'' and she cast her eyes down, her voice so low, so hoarse, he could barely hear her words. "I will be with the one I love, then.''

Varakov closed his eyes, folding the girl into his arms.

They would all die, he knew—unless he could find Rourke and Natalia—and soon.

Chapter Fifty-One

Rourke had placed the three motorcycles aboard the fighter bomber, Natalia and Paul—his left arm slung, useless because of the spear wound until it healed—having removed as much of the camouflage as necessary.

He started forward, seating himself behind the main console in the nose section, testing his electrical system.

Destroy Filmore Air Force base, fly to as near the Retreat as possible, then get the plane camouflaged once again. Go to the Retreat, get the truck, come back for the supplies, leave Paul to recuperate and read the note Natalia insisted he read, the note from her uncle. If it had been urgent, it was not urgent now, he thought.

So much time had elapsed.

Then regardless of the note, before doing whatever it was General Varakov was so insistent about—find his wife, his children.

Sarah—Michael—Annie—Rourke exhaled a long sigh, chewing down on his cigar as he watched the gauges rise. It was stuffy—but he didn't want to start the climate control systems panel yet. There was still more to check out.

What could Varakov want? he wondered. Perhaps Natalia's position had become untenable and Varakov merely wanted her with him—safe. Rourke smiled—he hardly considered himself safe, or anyone with him.

But whatever, the note would not be the important thing. It would be secondary. He would search Tennessee, search for Resistance units—perhaps one had seen something of a woman and two children. Were they still on horseback? he wondered.

He smiled as he thought of the animals—Tildie, his wife's, and Sam, his own, the big gray with the black mane and tail and four black stockings.

It would be good to ride with them again—to ride Sam, to ride with Sarah.

He could hear the thunder as it rumbled in the sky. He would maintain radio silence to avoid accidental Soviet detection. He imagined static would be unbearable at the higher altitudes anyway. He kept checking his instruments. . . .

Filmore Air Force base came into view as Rourke, flying low as he planned to do cross country, came over the ridge of rocks. He adjusted his altitude to match the lower level of the valley floor, beginning his attack run.

"John—if it will be easier," Natalia's voice came through his headset radio, "I can launch the missiles from my controls."

Rourke nodded in his helmet. "No—I'll do it," he told her, his face mask clouding a little as he spoke. He overflew the field, climbing slightly to bank, mentally picking his targets on the computer grids, verifying with the television optical unit mounted under the nose that the base was still untouched and the assault would be necessary. There were human figures on the ground—wildmen, from the quick look at them. There would be some left, wandering, leaderless.

Their loss would be necessary—and useful, too.

He finished the bank, rolling over into a level flight path, checking his angle of attack indicator, his approach indexer, these mounted to his left front.

He reached out his gloved left hand, his right on the control stick, adjusting the switches on his air combat maneuver panel.

Rourke overflew the field again, climbing to bank, the rollover, then leveling off, his weapons systems panel controls armed. He checked the wing sweep indicator on his lower left.

"Going in," he said into the headset microphone built into his helmet.

He poised his left hand over the controls—he fired, a Phoenix missile targeting toward the ammo dump, the ammo dump suddenly exploding as he launched the second Phoenix, the armory erupting into a fireball. He did a slight rollover, banking to port, leveling off, loosing a cluster of 24Mk82 580-pound mass iron bombs, pulling his nose up, the plane light now as the weight of the pylons was gone from the wings, the bombs impacting and exploding as he swung his visual scanning television monitor rearward, watching it as he nosed up and climbed.

The runway was gone—there would be a crater

there once the smoke and debris and flame cleared —there would be no runway.

He switched the TFR, the terrain-following radar helping him as he dropped his altitude, to maintain a constant elevation regardless of the ripples and rises in the terrain.

"We're going home," Rourke said quietly.

Neither Paul Rubenstein nor Natalia answered him.

But he hadn't expected they would.

Chapter Fifty-Two

The Womb radar system—once the Mt. Thunder North American Air Defense Command Center Radar in the Colorado Rockies—showed a blip.

The technician punched the alert button, in the next instant his supervisor was beside him.

"Comrade Lieutenant—this is not in our approach paths for the field—flying low—a TFR flight—hypersonic—the pattern of the blip matches that of the American F-111—perhaps a variant."

He looked up at the lieutenant, taking his eyes off the blip for an instant.

"I will contact weapons—" The lieutenant picked up the red telephone receiver from its red cradle on the console.

"Radar has a confirmed American blip—F-111-type fighter attack bomber—request use of the particle beam weapons system. Yes, comrade—I will hold."

The technician watched his blip.

"It is moving fast, comrade—at approximately eight hundred miles per hour—"

"Comrade—we are losing the blip," he heard the lieutenant say.

"It is leaving my screen, Comrade Lieutenant," the technician said, watching the green blip fading to his left.

"Very good, comrade," and the technician heard the receiver click down to its carriage—he didn't take his eyes from the radar screen to watch it.

"Use of the particle beam weapons system was denied."

"The blip is lost, Comrade Lieutenant," the technician said.

"Let him live—at least for a bit longer." And the lieutenant laughed.

The technician kept his eyes on the screen—perhaps there would be another one—or if this blip returned, to attack the field, perhaps then the particle beam weapons system would be employed. He had seen the test when it had been installed days earlier at the Womb. The pencil-thin beam of light, barely visible—the drone aircraft had been vaporized, disintegrated—it had been the most impressive thing he had ever seen. He watched his dull radar panel again—nothing but supply craft for the Womb.

Chapter Fifty-Three

Sarah Rourke walked slowly past the burned farmhouse—it was so much like her own home—gone.

And now John was gone again—with the Russian woman—the name of the woman, the submarine commander had told her, was Major Natalia Anastasia Tiemerovna. She rolled the name, trying to taste it—she hadn't asked if the woman was beautiful. And the man he traveled with—Paul Rubenstein. She had no doubt that if the woman—this major—were the woman of either John Rourke or the man Paul Rubenstein that she was John's woman. She smiled for a moment, stopping her walk—what woman, given the option to be, would not be John Rourke's woman.

Except perhaps herself—it had crossed her mind more than once before the Night of The War. But divorce was a word she could never say to him—she loved him too much, and he loved her.

Perhaps he thought she was dead—but then why did he tell Gundersen he would be searching for her?

There were questions to ask—but they would

come when he found her. She decided something. The Resistance fought an important fight—she was part of it. She would stay with Critchfield and the others—and Bill would someday be back. She would stay with them, fight—and someday John Rourke would find her.

"Someday," she said.

She felt silly—and she started to cry. She kept walking.

Chapter Fifty-Four

They had left the truck, the concentrations of Russians on the only roads through the mountains too great for them to risk the noise. Camouflaged more than a mile back, Bill Mulliner and his three men walked on. It would be risky—no code words or countersigns existed within the Resistance—it was not even an organization. Once they encountered the Resistance, he would have to rely on convincing the leader—reportedly a man named Koenigsburg—that Pete Critchfield had indeed sent him, that the messages he carried—all verbal—were indeed those of Critchfield and of President Chambers and Reed, Chambers' intelligence aide.

He let out a long sigh—he wondered if, by the time he did eventually get back to the new headquarters, Mrs. Rourke would already be gone as they had thought. He hoped someday to see her again, to meet a woman like her.

He walked on, his right fist on the pistol grip of his M-16. She would remember him, he knew—if for no other reason than his father's pistol, the Trapper .45, which he had given her. But he hoped for other reasons, too. . . .

Rourke stepped back from the plane—it was, once again, well camouflaged. But from the air only. To land the craft he had selected the only spot available, and there was little peripheral wooded area nearby to which he could "snuggle" the plane to obscure it at least partially on the ground. He had made the plane tamperproof—unless someone happened by with a parts replacement kit for an F-111 and a machine shop to alter parts, for this was a prototype model based on the F-111 only—it would be impossible to get it off the ground.

He turned, walking toward Natalia and Rubenstein, Rubenstein already straddling his Harley, Natalia standing beside hers, her motor not yet started either.

"Not much more than an hour to the Retreat from here," Rourke called out.

"And then rest for Paul—"

"And for you," Rourke told her.

"I will help you—"

"Paul will need those dressings changed at least once a day—he can't do it himself," Rourke told Natalia. "Besides—I have to get moving fast. You're still a little weak from the operation—you know that yourself."

"I am not," she insisted.

"All right—you're not," he smiled. He straddled the Low Rider. "Ready?" he asked both of them.

Rubenstein nodded, starting his engine, Natalia

mounting her machine. "Ready," she said, glaring at him.

Rourke gunned the Harley ahead—there was a shortcut he thought he could use, taking him through the park that surrounded Anna Ruby Falls outside Helen, Georgia.

He aimed the Harley's fork toward it. . . .

The body was a fresh kill, or so it seemed, Bill Mulliner thought, peering through the field glasses, down onto the bridge that crossed the rocky stream at the base of the falls.

He scanned the binoculars up toward the falls themselves, estimating the drop at well more than a hundred feet—and he had always been a poor judge of exact distances.

He scanned the area to the far side of the falls, high rocks and a muddy path leading up into woods.

He looked back to the bridge—the man was an American, not looking like a Brigand—too clean, Bill Mulliner thought.

Then he saw the movement, almost dropping his binoculars, refocusing them. On a flat rock about fifty feet further downstream beyond the bridge and the falls was another body—American-seeming, too. And the body still had life in it.

"We've gotta go down there," Bill Mulliner whispered hoarsely to his three men.

"Bullshit—probably Brigands or somethin'," one man, taller than Bill by a head or more, bearded, rasped.

"The man on the rock is alive." Bill Mulliner

233

peered through his binoculars—as the body moved again, he saw the face. He had seen it once before, in passing, during a Resistance attack. The man would not remember him—but he remembered the face, the man who owned it—Koenigsberg, the Resistance leader he had come to find.

"That's Koenigsberg."

"Then we go home," the bearded man murmured.

Bill Mulliner put down his glasses and looked at the older, taller man.

"We can go around and circle to the other side to our left, or we can go around to our right and come up the gorge, or we can head straight down—either way of the first two will take at least a half-hour. He'll be dead by then, maybe, and all three ways we're wide in the open for anybody lookin' down at us from the other side of them rocks. There's a human being—a fellow Resistance fighter, down there. We go get him. And any man who's too cowardly to go and help—well, damn well stay here and cover me—or just run."

Bill Mulliner swept the far side of the gorge behind the falls with the binoculars again. He saw no movement except for a squirrel moving almost lazily up a tree trunk. It was like the deerwoods on a smoky afternoon.

"Let's go—those that are goin'," and Bill Mulliner pushed himself up, the binoculars swinging from his neck, the M-16 in his hands. He started out of the rocks and toward the long, steep, dirt-and-rock side of the gorge. It would be a hard climb down, he thought.

"Wait up," one of the men called in a loud stage

whisper, and Bill Mulliner turned around.

Rifle shots—the bearded man who had complained fell flat backwards and never moved. Bill wheeled, his M-16 coming up, something hammering into his chest as there was another burst of gunfire. There was a scream from behind him as he heard more of the gunfire.

Bill fell backward, hitting his head on a rock, shaking his head to clear it. He looked down—his chest was bleeding, bubbles of blood pumping from over his right lung. "Jesus—I'm shot," he said to himself.

He pushed himself to his feet, stumbling. There was more gunfire, but this time from behind him. "Come on, Billy—come on," the voice of Thad Fricks came to him.

Thad was alive, Bill thought. He turned, trying to move away from the edge of the rocks. Another burst of gunfire—Thad Fricke's rifle went off and he fell, disappearing into the trees.

Bill Mulliner gasped, a pain gripping his chest.

A single rifle shot, and already he was falling, his left leg burning, his face and his hands skidding along the rocks as he fell downward, his rifle gone, his head bumping against a pine tree stump, a clump of brush—a handhold, but he slipped from it and fell, sliding again, rolling, rolling, rolling.

"Sweet Jesus!" he screamed. . . .

"Those shots were from the falls," Rourke almost whispered, his bike stopped near the top of a hilly rise.

"What do you think, John?" Rubenstein asked.

"Whatever you want to do," Natalia murmured.

235

"Can't be too many—not too many shots—sound like assault rifles—but too high-pitched for AK-47s —not your people," Rourke said, looking at Natalia.

"Agreed—.223s—all of them."

Rourke gunned the Harley—"Let's go," and let out the machine, starting ahead, up a gully and alongside a row of yearling Georgia pines and then into a sparse woods, hearing the roar of Rubenstein's and Natalia's bikes behind him, feeling the throb of the Harley's engine between his legs.

He hit the top of the rise and bounced a hummock of dirt, seeing the drop off into the gorge ahead, slowing the bike, braking, kicking down the stand, dismounting, the CAR-15 in his hands. He saw three bodies on the ground as he ran toward the edge, hearing Paul's and Natalia's bikes stopping behind him.

At the bottom of the steep side of the gorge there were bodies—one on a bridge across the stream at the base of the falls, still another on rocks there beneath the bridge and fifty feet or so beyond. And a third— the third body and the second body still moved. And there were men—Brigands—moving down from the far side of the gorge, what looked from the distance like M-16s in their hands—five of them.

They had not heard the motorcycles coming, Rourke realized—the steady, drowning roar of the falls itself obscuring the noise.

They were Brigands—Brigands—the cut of the men, the dirt, the faces, the way they moved. He saw the lead man raise his M-16 and fire into the man on the rocks who had still moved—the man moved no more. They were Brigands—cold-blooded murderers.

Rourke shouldered the CAR-15, ripping away the scope covers—he was cold-blooded, too.

He flicked the safety, pumping a two-shot burst into the man who had just murdered. The body fell, Rourke shifting the scope, finding another target, killing.

There was gunfire from beside him—Natalia's M-16, Rubenstein's German MP-40—Paul had called it a Schmeisser so long Rourke thought of it that way too now.

The bodies fell.

All five were down. Rourke shifted his rifle—one shot to each man, to each head—five dead.

"John—the one at the base of the grade here—a boy with red hair—he's moving."

Rourke handed her his rifle, "Take the bikes and start along the side here until you can climb down safely—watch your stitches and watch Paul's arm. I'll go this way."

"All right," she whispered.

Rourke—his rifle with Natalia—started to the edge, found a spot that looked the least steep, and started down, slipping onto his rear end, sliding, catching himself, skidding on the heels of his boots, getting to a standing position, running to keep up with his momentum, slipping, falling back, skidding, then getting his balance.

He half jumped, half fell, but was standing—in a crouch—as he hit the bottom of the gorge. He picked his way across the spray-licked, moss-greened rocks, toward the red-haired boy, the roar of the falls louder now.

No other body moved—but the boy moved.

Rourke skidded across a low boulder—blood there—and dropped to his knees beside the boy.

"Easy, son," Rourke said, raising the boy's head—the hand he held the head in was sticky and wet with blood.

"Ambushed us," the boy gasped.

"It's all right—we got 'em for you—Brigands—"

"Yeah—we—we call 'em that—that, too," the boy sighed.

"Don't try to talk—don't—"

"Gotta help—help the man—the man on the rocks—"

"He's dead," Rourke whispered. "One of the Brigands got him—I killed the guy who did it—rest easy." He wondered if it would help the boy to say that he was a doctor—for his skills as a doctor would not—blood loss, a lung that seemed collapsed—there was a chest wound that did not suck—and obviously, from just a superficial examination, numerous bones broken. The boy was dying. He decided to say it anyway, to lie that the boy would live, or could. "I'm a doctor, son—I'll do what I can for you to make you comfortable." He couldn't lie.

"I'm dyin'—you're a doc—you know that," and the boy coughed up a slimy mixture of blood and spittle.

"I'm a doctor—and I know that," Rourke nodded, holding the boy closer. "You with the Resistance?"

"Yeah—you, too?"

"No—I'm with some friends—a man and a woman—they're coming," and Rourke heard footfalls

238

on the rocks behind him. He glanced back—it was Natalia only.

"John—I left Paul—the climb was too steep with his arm."

"John?" The boy hissed the word.

"Yeah, son—my name's John—"

"A doctor?"

"Yeah—"

"John Rourke," the boy gasped.

"I don't know you," Rourke said, studying the boy's face more closely.

"Sarah," the boy gasped. "Boy Michael—a little girl—Annie—"

Rourke tightened his left hand's grip on the boy's shoulder—"My wife and children—you've—"

"Cunningham—Cunningham horse farm—near Mt. Eagle, Tennessee," the boy gasped.

"Mt. Eagle," Rourke whispered. "You're—you're—Mulliner—the red-haired boy with the gun that night at the door—the Mulliner farm."

"Bill Mulliner," the boy coughed. "Bill Mulliner—tell my mom—tell her I love her—tell her—and—tell Mrs. Rourke—good—good. . . ."

The boy's eyes stayed open, blood drooled from the right corner of his mouth as his head sagged away.

"Good-bye," Rourke said for the dead boy, and he looked up into Natalia's blue eyes. She closed her eyes and said nothing.

"Sarah," Rourke whispered.

NEL BESTSELLERS

Orbit	*Thomas Block*	£1.95
The White Plague	*Frank Herbert*	£2.50
Shrine	*James Herbert*	£2.25
Christine	*Stephen King*	£2.50
The War Hound and the World's Pain	*Michael Moorcock*	£2.50
Spellbinder	*Harold Robbins*	£2.50
The Longest Day	*Cornelius Ryan*	£1.95
The Case of Lucy B.	*Lawrence Sanders*	£2.50
Acceptable Losses	*Irwin Shaw*	£1.95
Crabs' Moon	*Guy N. Smith*	£1.75
I, The Jury	*Mickey Spillane*	£1.25
The Seven Minutes	*Irving Wallace*	£2.25

All these books are available at your local bookshop or newsagent, or can be ordered direct from the publisher. Just tick the titles you want and fill in the form below.

NEL P.O. BOX 11, FALMOUTH TR10 9EN, CORNWALL

Postage Charge:

U.K. Customers 55p for the first book plus 22p for the second book and 14p for each additional book ordered to a maximum charge of £1.75.

B.F.P.O. & EIRE Customers 55p for the first book plus 22p for the second book and 14p for the next 7 books; thereafter 8p per book.

Overseas Customers £1.00 for the first book and 25p per copy for each additional book.

Please send cheque or postal order (no currency).

Name ....

Address ....

....

Title ....

While every effort is made to keep prices steady, it is sometimes necessary to increase prices at short notice. New English Library reserve the right to show on covers and charge new retail prices which may differ from those advertised in the text or elsewhere. (B)